BRICK
A Lords of Carnage MC Romance

DAPHNE LOVELING

This book is a work of fiction.

Any similarity to persons living or dead is purely coincidental.

CONTENTS

To you.

DAPHNE LOVELING

1
SYDNEY

"You don't have kolaches?" the elderly man on the other side of the counter huffs at me.

A frown of confusion crosses my face. "What's a kolache?" I ask him.

The man rolls his watery blue eyes. "All these baked goods," he says disdainfully, nodding toward my display case. "And no kolaches."

"I'm sorry." I try for my most patient tone. "If you can explain to me what a kolache is, maybe I can point you to something in the case that would be similar."

He scoffs. "Nothing similar in *there*." He fixes me with a withering look, as though he's half-expecting me to die of shame right on the spot. "I'll just have a cup of black coffee with some creamer."

"Sure, thing," I say brightly, reaching for a cup. I fill it with hot, freshly brewed coffee and set it down on the counter. "There's milk and cream in those carafes over there," I say, pointing over toward the condiment bar, "so you can pour it in yourself."

"You don't have any Coffee Mate?" His face goes from sour to incredulous.

Oh, lord.

"No, I'm sorry, we don't." I try to make myself sound *deeply* apologetic. "There's cream, two percent, and skim," I tell him. "And refills are free! You can help yourself. Right next to the cream and milk."

I don't know why I was hoping that might brighten his mood, but it definitely does not.

He snorts. "Figures."

I don't even know what he means by that, but I'm not about to ask. Apparently, I have sunk to exactly the depths of immorality he expects from the owner of a fancy-schmancy coffee shop.

I ring him up, trying not to look apologetic or defensive when I tell him the total. It's clear from his expression he thinks it's an exorbitant amount to pay. Thankfully, though, he seems sick enough of me by now not to bother arguing. He pulls a crumpled bill out of his pants pocket and slides it toward me, then waits in silence until I give him his change.

With a loud *harrumph*, he stalks off without leaving so much as a penny as a tip. Of course.

My dissatisfied customer hobbles to the condiment bar and gingerly pours in a thin trickle of skim milk, as though a single drop too much might just poison him. Then, he shoots me one last disdainful look, and goes over to join the two perfectly pleasant old men I served a few minutes earlier, who are occupying a nice sunny table by the window.

I take in a deep breath and slowly let it out, then plaster my best customer-service smile on my face and turn to the next person in line. As much as I hate to admit it, I'm remarkably thin-skinned when it comes to interactions like this. But, as I remind myself for the hundredth time, it's par for the course in customer service jobs. *You knew what you were getting into when you opened the Golden Cup, Syd. So suck it up, buttercup.*

And it's true. When I opened up the first and only full-service coffee shop in Tanner Springs, I figured I'd have more than a few customers on a learning curve at first. If I had any customers at all, that is. Fortunately, I seem to have been correct that the residents of this small town would welcome a new place to congregate over good coffee and homemade pastries. My worst fear was that no one would ever come into the shop, and that I'd spend my days wistfully looking out the window, watching all the money I've invested in this place spiral the drain. Thankfully, that has not come to pass.

But opening this shop hasn't been without its bumps in the road. And one of the downsides has been that some of my older clientele — Grumpy Kolache Guy, for example — is more used to diner coffee. And diner prices. They can be a little tough to please, to say the least.

I busy myself with my morning tasks and helping other customers, noting with some satisfaction that Grumpy Guy helps himself to refills on coffee not once, but twice. The sour expression never leaves his face, though. I'll be surprised if he ever comes back to my shop again after today.

The thought doesn't exactly fill me with sadness.

It's a little after seven-thirty in the morning when, right on schedule, the morning rush begins. Every weekday, Monday through Friday, there's a sudden onslaught from now until almost eight-thirty. A steady stream of humanity files through the front door of the shop, each of them seeking to feed their caffeine and sugar addictions. There are professionally dressed adults hustling in on their way to work, and students on their way to high school before first bell. Many of them I recognize by now, and I do my best to remember details from past conversations and ask after their families. They seem to appreciate the attention, and I know the routine of our little morning chats is one of the reasons they'll keep coming back for more.

I work as quickly as I can, making sure the line doesn't get too long. Business has definitely been picking up in the last few weeks, and it's getting harder for me to handle the morning rush by myself. I've been putting off hiring someone to help me out in the mornings, even though at this point, I can probably just about afford it. Truth be told, I sort of like the rush-rush of working these mornings by myself. It makes me feel like Superwoman to handle it all without getting in the weeds.

I'm feverishly steaming milk for an order of espresso drinks when the bell to the shop sounds. I look up to see the familiar figure of my only employee, Hailey, walking in.

"Hey, what are you doing here?" I ask her as she slips behind the counter. "Your shift isn't until this afternoon."

"Math test," she replies, pulling down a to-go cup. "I need the caffeine."

Hailey helps herself to an iced latte while I'm serving other customers. "Also, I wanted to let you know I'm going to be a little late coming in today after school," she explains in an annoyed voice. "My friend Melissa talked me into being on some stupid Senior Activities Committee."

"No problem," I say. "Just get here as soon as you can."

She rolls her pale blue eyes and blows her dyed lilac-colored bangs out of her face. "Believe me, I will. You're my excuse for cutting out of there as soon as possible."

I laugh as I ring up a customer. "Why are you doing it, then, if you don't want to?"

Hailey shrugs. "I don't know. What can I say? I'm a giver."

Just then, the phone rings. *Shit.* "Do you have time to grab that, Hailey?" I ask.

"Sure," she says, picking up the receiver. "Golden Cup Coffee, this is Hailey…"

The line to be served is six deep now. This is the busiest I've ever been during a morning rush so far. It's just a regular Friday morning, and I can't think of any particular reason there should be so many people today. I feel a little buzz of elation at my success, but quickly squash it down because there are customers to attend to. I cast a worried glance at the pastry case. Already I'm running low on muffins, and I wonder whether I'll need to start making more.

Hailey speaks a few more words into the phone and hangs up. The shop bell tinkles again as I straighten from retrieving a lemon poppyseed muffin from the case.

"Who was it?" I ask her.

She turns to answer me, but then her gaze shifts toward the door. Her eyes widen in surprise. "Holy cow," she murmurs. "Who the hell is *that?*"

2
SYDNEY

I glance over to see who she's looking at, and almost immediately the skin on my arms tightens with goosebumps.

The man standing in the doorway is so massive that he blocks almost all the light coming through it. Looking at him, the first word that comes to mind is *dark*. His hair is black as night, cropped short and no-nonsense in an almost military style. The dark shadow of a beard accentuates his square jaw. Tattoos line his arms below the taut sleeves of his black T-shirt.

As I try not to stare, the man's deep brown eyes lock on mine. He gives me a lazy, sexy smirk. I draw in a sharp breath and give him a quick nod, then look away.

For the past two weeks, this mass of a man has been coming into my shop about every other day. He always orders a black coffee to go, and sometimes a pastry. He rides a low, black motorcycle whose engine rumble I can recognize immediately by now. It's a testament to how busy I am today that I didn't hear him pull up.

The worn leather vest he always wears is adorned with various patches. They tell me he's a member of a motorcycle club called the Lords of Carnage. One patch on his chest says, "Brick," which I assume is his name, or a nickname. Another says the word, "Enforcer."

I know all of this because I've spent the last couple of weeks staring everywhere but at his face.

Hailey gives a low whistle. "He's crazy hot," she whispers.

"And a little old for you," I murmur back.

"Well, maybe," she concedes. "But not for *you*."

"He's a little… tattoo-ey for me," I reply, keeping my voice light. "Besides, he's a customer."

She snorts. "It's not like there's some sort of *rule* against hooking up with someone you sell coffee to."

"Hailey," I warn. "Drop it. I have a business to run. And I am not in the market for a boyfriend."

"Psh," she dismisses me with a wave of her hand. "Everyone says that. But everyone is."

I shake my head but don't try to argue with her. I know the less I protest, the quicker she'll drop the subject and move on. And I am *really* not interested in discussing my love life, or lack thereof, with a high school student. Or the relative sexiness of my motorcycle-riding regular customer. Hailey is seventeen going on thirty, and far too nosey for her own good.

Also, maybe a little too perceptive.

Because deep down inside, I have to admit that his tattoos are *super* hot.

Hailey takes her cell phone out of her back pocket and glances at the time. "I have to go," she mutters. "See you this afternoon." She pulls out a couple of bills, and starts to put them on the counter, but I stop her.

"On the house," I tell her. "Good luck with the math test."

"Thanks," she grins, and flicks her eyes toward Brick. "Good luck with Mr. Hottie."

I resist the urge to reply, and go back to serving customers. The rush seems to be slowing now, thankfully. No one has gotten in line behind Brick yet. I make lattes and mochas as fast as I can take orders. The steam from the machine heats me up, and I start to perspire. I can feel Brick's eyes on me, and have to resist the urge to reach up and smooth my hair. A trickle of sweat slides down between my breasts.

By the time he gets to the head of the line, I've over-rehearsed our conversation in my head enough times that I hope I'll manage not to sound like a complete dork.

"Good morning," I say in an overly chatty tone. "The usual?"

He gives me a panty-melting half-grin. "Am I that predictable?" he asks, his voice a deep rumble.

"Medium dark roast, to go, no room for cream, in your to-go cup," I rattle off automatically. "A blueberry muffin if you're feeling crazy."

He laughs, a low, sexy growl that starts way down in his throat. It reminds me weirdly of the sound of his motorcycle engine. "Shit, I guess I *am* that predictable," he says, deadpan, and hands me his travel mug. "Maybe I need to branch out a little. What do you recommend?" He glances over at the pastry case.

"Well…" I consider the options. "I just made some apricot-ginger scones. It's my first day offering them."

The scone is kind of a challenge, actually. In my experience, big, muscular types like him tend to have a congenital allergy to anything they think of as girly or "foo-foo." It's almost like they think it will make their testicles shrivel up and fall off. Scones *definitely* qualify as one of those things. But to my surprise, he considers it for a moment and then nods. "Sounds kind of good. Okay, you got it." He glances toward the tables. "And I'll take my scone for here today."

"Oh… um, sure," I say. He's *never* stayed here to eat before. I realize I've sort of been counting down the seconds until he leaves the shop and I can relax. "In that case, just have a seat." I give him my best professional smile, wondering if it's too big and I look like a maniac. "I'll bring the coffee and scone to your table in a second."

He pays in cash and stuffs a couple of bills in the tip jar, then goes to sit at a small table in the corner that has a newspaper sitting on it. As he settles in, the three old men stand up from their table and get ready to leave. One of them, a rotund man with a Wilford Brimley look and a crown of silvery white hair, gives me a friendly wave.

"Thank you much, miss," he calls to me as they reach the door. "We'll be back again soon!"

"I hope everything was tasty," I call back as I walk toward Brick's table with his scone and coffee.

Grouchy Guy sniffs as he follows his friends out the door. "I still say, this is no kind of bakery without kolaches," he announces to no one in particular, jutting out his chin defiantly.

Brick looks up at me with a frown.

"What the hell's a kolache?" he asks.

3
BRICK

This girl's a fucking knockout.

I knew that the first time I saw her, of course. But up close, without a counter between us, I'm almost blown away by the sight of her.

I came into the Golden Cup for the first time a couple weeks ago, after a night of pretty intense partying with the Lords. I was hung over and on my way to the clubhouse for an early morning run Rock had set up. My coffee maker was broken, my ass was dragging, and I felt like shit. Then on my way through downtown, I noticed the new coffee shop I'd driven by a few times, and decided to stop in.

Turned out the coffee was damn good. But the chick serving it to me was even better.

I bought a new coffee maker the next day, but it's still sitting on my kitchen counter in the box it came in. Since then, I've been coming in a few times a week for a cup to go on the way to the garage. Shit, this girl's even got me eating goddamn *muffins*. I've taken a fair amount of ribbing from the brothers about it, but fuck them. Those muffins are *good*.

Today, when I come in, there's a bigger line than I've ever seen. Coffee girl is working like a madwoman behind the counter. I'm last in line, but I don't mind waiting. It means I can stare at her ass while she works the espresso machine.

By the time I get to the front of the line, there's no one behind me, and the shop has pretty much cleared out except for a trio of old dudes by the window.

The hot redhead cocks her head at me and gives me a saucy smirk of recognition. "The usual?" she asks.

"Am I that predictable?"

"Medium dark roast, to go, no room for cream, in your to-go cup. A blueberry muffin if you're feeling crazy."

I'm due at the shop, to help Hawk finish up work on a bike that a customer wants to pick up later today. But for some reason, instead of taking my usual order to go, I decide on the spur of the moment to sit down and stay for a while.

"What the hell's a kolache?" I repeat as she sets my coffee and a scone in front of me.

13

"Huh?" The girl's eyes flick from the doorway down to me, then back again. "Oh," she shrugs. "I guess it's some kind of pastry," she says. "He seemed really upset that I didn't have any in the case."

Up close like this, I notice there's a sprinkling of freckles across the bridge of her nose. I've always been a sucker for freckles. While she's still distracted, I take a moment to stare at the swell of her breasts under the simple white T-shirt she's wearing. Her thick auburn hair is pulled back from her face into a high ponytail, exposing the creamy skin of her neck. I want to wrap my hand around it and tug her head back, just a little. Just enough to see the pulse point as her heartbeat speeds up.

My cock thickens and strains against my zipper.

"He seems like the kind of guy who makes a hobby out of being pissed," I remark.

She nods, and turns back to me. "Maybe," she agrees. "I just don't like it when I feel like I've disappointed someone. You know?"

I shrug. "Can't please everyone," I say.

She smirks. "Well, pleasing everyone is kind of what makes a successful business."

I break off a bite of the scone and put it in my mouth. I chew for a couple of seconds, then raise my eyebrows. "Damn. This is good."

She laughs outright. "That was fake as hell. You just said that right on cue to make me feel better."

I shake my head. "I don't say shit I don't mean."

She eyes me speculatively and quirks up her strawberry lips, considering. "Not sure I buy that."

"Do I look like a people-pleaser?" I ask sardonically.

She laughs again, throwing her head back and exposing her throat. *Fuck.* My cock is instantly hard as a bat. I don't even know why a throat would do this to me. But hers does. I want to nip at the skin. I want to feel the vibrations of her moan against my lips as I tease her. I want to hear her breath catch in her throat as her pulse starts to race.

I shift uncomfortably, thankful for the table hiding my obvious erection. "Name's Brick," I say thickly.

"I know." Still smiling, she nods toward the patch on my cut.

"Right," I chuckle. For a second, neither of us says anything. "So," I prompt, "This is the point where you say, 'Pleased to meet you, Brick. My name's…'"

Her expression falters for just a second. She bites her strawberry lip. "Sydney," she says finally.

I listen to the music of her name. It's unique. It seems to suit her.

"As in Australia?"

"Exactly." She seems surprised. "With a Y. I mean, with two Y's. S-y-d."

I nod.

"Is Brick your real name?" she asks.

"It's a road name. A nickname," I clarify.

"Oh." After a moment, she asks, "What's your real name?"

I don't know why I don't just tell her it's none of her business. I think about it.

A few seconds pass.

"Gavin," I finally grunt.

She takes a moment to consider this.

"Pleased to meet you, *Gavin*," she corrects.

I haven't heard anyone say my given name in a long time. It feels strange to hear it on her lips.

Not sure how I feel about it.

"You the owner here?" I say, to distract myself.

"Yeah." A small, proud smile shifts the corners of her mouth.

"The place seems to be doing pretty well," I remark. "It was busy in here today."

"Thanks. She flushes slightly with pleasure. "It seems like the morning rush just gets bigger every week."

"That's great. You must be doing something right."

"Maybe. Though, you wouldn't know it right now," she says with a rueful grin.

I glance around. We're alone in the shop.

"You're pretty young to own your own business," I observe. "You some kind of trust fund kid?"

She snorts. "Hardly."

"Witness protection plan, then," I joke.

Something in her face contracts. It's almost instantaneous, and abrupt. "Look, I don't think it's really any of your business, do you?" she half-snaps.

"Jesus, don't get your panties in a twist," I protest, raising my eyebrows. I don't know what button I've pushed, but I've clearly rankled her. Shit, maybe she really *is* in WITSEC. "I meant it as a compliment."

"Really?" she retorts with a cold scowl. "Talking about my *panties* is supposed to be a compliment?"

Fuck, the temperature in this place just went down ten degrees. She's got a temper on her, that's for sure.

"No, not that, for fuck's sake," I say in frustration. "Look, it's just an expression. I'm sorry, okay?" I hold up one hand in a truce signal. "If it makes you feel any better, I'd say it to a guy, too."

Just then a phone rings in the back. She frowns at me and shakes her head. "Excuse me," she murmurs, and moves off back behind the counter. I get another good look at her ass, and also her legs in her tight little jeans.

And wonder what kind of panties she's wearing.

While she's talking on the phone, I pull out my cell and look something up.

"It's Czech," I say as soon as she hangs up.

"What?" She's confused. Good. Maybe I can distract her from the panties thing before she remembers to get riled up again.

"Kolaches," I say. I wave my cell at her, then read from the screen. "Says here they're 'a type of pastry that holds a dollop of fruit, rimmed by a puffy pillow of supple dough.' Apparently, it's a thing from Eastern Europe. Czechoslovakia."

She wrinkles her nose. "Oh."

"I guess they're a thing around here. Never heard of it, though."

"Me, neither," she frowns. "Though I'm not from here originally."

"I gathered. Most people from around here seem to know everyone else. Where are you from?"

"Um." She raises a distracted hand to her ponytail and starts to play with the end. "New Jersey." Her eyes flick away from me. Huh. She *really* doesn't seem to like personal questions. "You?"

"New York. Upstate. Near Seneca Lake."

"Oh, wow, I've been there!" The sullen expression leaves her face as her eyes turn suddenly luminous. "My dad took me once. It's beautiful!"

"Yeah," I grunt. Objectively, she's not wrong. My mind flashes on the crystalline lake of my childhood, and I imagine what it would look like to an outsider: Peaceful. Calm. Idyllic.

Pretty much the exact opposite of my childhood.

I let out a little snort as I think about my main memories of living there. My drunk-ass piece of shit father. My mother, who eventually started drinking even more than he did. The foster families I ended up living with because she couldn't take care of my sister and me after my dad went to prison. The goddamn shit show that was our joke of a family. A bitter taste rises up in my gorge, but I push it back down and take a swig of my coffee.

If Sydney notices any change in me, she doesn't let on. "Why did you leave?" she asks innocently, and then seems to think better of it. "Sorry," she says with an apologetic shrug. "That's really none of my business."

"No, it's okay." I set the cup down. I'm sure as hell not going to unpack my life story for her, but I'm used to giving people the cleaned-up version. Shit, maybe if I give her a couple details about me, she'll let her guard down a little bit and tell me more about herself. "I joined the military right out of high school," I tell her. "Marines. Ended up here in Tanner Springs after my tour was over because a buddy of mine is from here."

She lifts a brow. "You were a Marine? For how—"

An ear-splitting explosion and blinding flash of light cuts off her words, making her shriek with fright. It's coming from the kitchen.

And whatever it is, it just started a fire.

4
SYDNEY

"Jesus," Brick — *Gavin* — roars, jumping to his feet. "What the hell was that?"

"I don't know!" I cry, looking toward the back. My heart starts racing about a million miles an hour. It feels like it's about to burst through my chest.

He is across the room in a manner of seconds. Dazedly, I follow close behind, terrified but suddenly glad I'm not alone in the shop. In the kitchen, a column of flames has erupted from one of the burners of the stove. Gavin looks around and yanks the fire extinguisher from the wall. He pulls the pin, aims the nozzle, and squeezes the lever.

Nothing happens.

"Fuck," he shouts. "Where's your baking soda?"

I start to tell him, but then have a better idea. "Wait!" I cry. "Get that lid over there!" He looks to where I'm pointing. I grab an oven glove and gingerly reach out to turn off the burner, and Gavin takes the large, flat lid and tosses it over the pan.

And just like that, the fire goes out, as quickly as it started.

"Holy shit," I gasp, leaning over. I put my hands on my knees and take a few deep breaths, willing myself not to hyperventilate.

Gavin sets the extinguisher on the counter. "Why the hell don't you have a working extinguisher in here?" he rasps.

Truth be told, I didn't know the extinguisher didn't work. It was fine when the fire marshal tested it out during the inspection. But Gavin talking to me like I'm some kind of stupid child, and I *hate* it when people talk to me like that. Especially men.

"It would have contaminated the entire kitchen if you'd used that," I pant, and take another deep breath to calm myself.

"Who the fuck cares?" he growls. "This whole place could have burned down. That would have been pretty goddamn 'contaminated,' too."

"Well, it didn't," I shoot back angrily. "So we're fine."

"Jesus Christ…" he runs a rough hand through his dark hair, looking like he is contemplating strangling me.

"Look." I reach over, leaning in toward him, and pick up a small metal object from the counter. "Here's the culprit." I hold out my hand so he can see it. It looks kind of like a large bullet with one end exploded.

"It's a nitrous oxide cartridge," I explain. "For the whipped cream dispenser. I must have left it on the stove top somehow. I guess it got too close to the flames and exploded."

He stares at it for a second, then looks over at the wall — which has a nitrous-oxide-sized dent in it at about chest level. "And that's where it hit when it flew," he says, pointing to the dent. For the first time, I notice that the skin on the back of his left hand is deeply scarred, like burns that have healed. The scarring continues halfway up his forearm, where it's partially obscured by an elaborate tattoo, of a skull half in shadow.

I hold the cartridge up to the dent he's pointing at and compare them. "Yeah, I bet you're right," I say. "I don't remember that dent being there before."

"Jesus," he mutters. "What the fuck were you doing, Sydney, leaving that thing lying around? What do you think that fucking cartridge would have done to you if you'd been in here?"

"Oh, calm down," I snap. "Seriously, it's no big deal. Nothing bad happened." He's making me feel like an idiot, and that just makes me madder.

"It could have taken out your eye. Or worse."

I let out a snort. "Oh, my God, lighten up! You sound like someone's grandmother."

"Goddamnit, I'm serious!" he grabs me by the arm and pulls me toward him. I'm so stunned I don't even think to pull away. "What if that thing had hit you in the chest, Sydney? If it could put a dent like that in the wall, what would it have done to you? What if it had hit you here?" His thumb grazes the skin just above the V of my T-shirt. "Or here?"

"I…" I stammer. The shock of his touch, so intimate, sends a jolt through me that sends everything into sharp relief. With him this close, his black eyes staring at me intensely, I'm a little bit scared, and also very, very aware that I'm completely alone with a man I barely know. A man who absolutely radiates sex and power. I can feel my body stiffen, even as heat begins to grow between my legs.

He must feel that he's frightened me, because a second later he loosens his grip on my wrist and pulls back just a little.

"Fuck," he mutters, and shakes his head. "Look, I'm sorry. But Jesus. You could be on your way to the emergency room right now. You get that, don't you?"

He's right, of course. If I'd been in the kitchen just now, I could have gotten seriously hurt. Burned, or worse. I've been trying to downplay it all, but thinking about how close I came to a life-changing accident sends a tremor of belated adrenaline through me. Suddenly, I feel just a little bit faint. My lip trembles, and I bite down on it so he won't notice. I take a deep breath.

"I get that I could have been hurt," I murmur, my voice almost cracking. "I just... prefer not to dwell on it. It didn't happen. Everything's fine. That's the important part. Okay?"

I'm expecting him to bark at me again. But he doesn't. He doesn't say anything, in fact.

He's still holding on to my wrist.

He pulls me just a little closer. I stare up at him — at his full, sensual lips. My skin starts to buzz. My nipples harden under my shirt.

I stop breathing. I think he does, too.

Gavin bends toward me. I make a small noise in my throat as my eyelids start to flutter shut.

"Hello?" a voice calls from out in the shop. My lids fly open.

He doesn't move. His eyes remain locked on me. He's waiting to see what I'll do.

"Be right there!" I call back. Wordlessly, I pull my wrist from his grasp and slip away from him, cheeks flushed pink.

The voice out in the shop belongs to Mrs. Bauer, who's come in with her little granddaughter in a stroller. With her, the mid-morning trickle of customers begins, and the tables begin to fill with the kinds of customers who linger over conversation and pastries. Mostly, it's older ladies who come into the shop in pairs and threes, or young mothers pushing strollers in search of a little quiet time.

It feels like a mercy that the pace of people coming in is just steady enough that I can avoid having to face Gavin again, after what almost happened back in the kitchen.

Because something *was* about to happen. And like an idiot, I wasn't going to do a damn thing to stop it.

You would think that I'd have learned a lesson or two about avoiding dangerous men and sketchy situations, given that I've had plenty of experience sizing people up and figuring out which ones were a danger and which weren't. I came to Tanner Springs in the first place precisely to leave my past behind — including one very bad mistake — and start fresh somewhere new. You'd think I'd be better by now at not jumping into stupid situations where I suddenly realize I'm in over my head.

I feel Gavin's presence as he slips behind me and out from behind the counter. He grabs his travel mug from his table and leaves without saying goodbye. I'm mostly relieved.

And a little disappointed.

As I get Mrs. Bauer's coffee drink and help her little granddaughter pick out a cookie, I silently berate myself. *What were you thinking, letting a complete stranger get that close to you? You don't know the first thing about him, other than he likes coffee and rides a motorcycle. That's Self-Defense 101, Sydney. And you failed.*

I ignore the argumentative *second* voice in my head — the one that's telling me not to be ridiculous. *He was just trying to help. Even though he was kind of an ass about it. You didn't even thank him, by the way.*

Yeah, scoffs the first voice. *That kind of 'help,' I definitely don't need.*

More customers come in. I take their orders and bring them drinks. All the while, the image of Gavin's face in my head. His look of anger mixed with concern as he grabbed my wrist.

The subtle way his eyes changed just before he bent toward me.

I shiver.

I can still feel the rough skin of his fingers as they clasped onto my wrist.

And the soft rasp of his thumb against the bare skin of my neck.

My eyes close for a moment as I imagine the soft pillow of his lips on mine.

I'm glad he's gone, I tell myself. *I'm glad nothing happened.*

So then why do I spend the rest of the day hoping it's him every time the shop bell sounds?

5
BRICK

Her eyes are gray-green. The color of moss in shadow.

They're all I can see as I ride over to the garage with what's left of my coffee.

Goddamn, though, did those eyes look like they wanted to slay me dead for implying she couldn't take care of herself. In spite of how pissed I still am, I almost chuckle at the memory. She is a feisty one — just like you'd guess from her mane of fiery red hair. Honestly, she does seem like she could probably hold her own against just about anybody. Something in her attitude makes me think she might have done a lot of fending for herself in her life. She's not like the sheltered little girls I see sometimes around Tanner Springs, making sex eyes at my brothers and me, and then fleeing in terror when we look back, like we're Satan's minions incarnate.

Sydney doesn't have any of that fake bullshit attitude about her. She's feminine as hell, without being girly. But at the same time, she doesn't have the same hardness around the eyes that some of the chicks who hang around the club have.

She definitely isn't a trust fund kid, like I originally wondered. Something tells me she didn't have an easy time of it, up there in Jersey. Which makes me wonder all the more how she ended up down here in eastern Ohio. What she was running to. Or running from.

I've never seen eyes the color of Sydney's before.

I want to see them flash at me. I like the challenge in them.

I want to see them flutter closed again, like they did just now when I was about to kiss her.

Even though she pissed me off mightily with her bullshit attitude about that nitrous oxide explosion.

My tires chew up the miles as I remember how much I wanted to momentarily shake some sense into that girl at her so-what reaction to the explosion. I wasn't kidding when I said she could have been seriously hurt. Even now, the last of the adrenaline is still thrumming in my veins. I'm still itching to do something — to *protect* her — even though the whole thing was already over practically before it started.

My hand closes tightly around the throttle as I think about it now. I know my surge of anger back there was because of the adrenaline rush from the explosion. It was just a chemical reaction, nothing more — a fight or flight response. But by the time I got back into the kitchen, the 'fight' was over. There was nothing to do. No one to punch. So I kind of took it out on Sydney instead. Which was kind of an asshole move.

I've never been a man to be comfortable in situations where I can't take action. I'm the club's Enforcer for a reason. I'm the guy that comes to see you when all the talking is over. In the club, I answer only to Rock, our prez. I make sure his orders are carried out. I'm the fist that punches for him. My fist maintains order in our world.

The explosion in the kitchen triggered some kind of caveman reaction in me, to protect Sydney. And when the danger was over — when the adrenaline had nowhere to go — being that close to her triggered another reaction. Something even more primal.

I shift on my seat, my cock still as hard as a damn bat. That girl's gonna be on my mind all morning. I can already tell.

Fuck.

I'm still feeling goddamn out of sorts as I walk into the garage.

"You're late," Hawk growls.

"Fuck you," I bark back. I grab my shop overalls and pull them on. Hawk grunts but doesn't say anything more. My bad mood notwithstanding, Hawk's one of the brothers I most respect in the club. He doesn't take bullshit, and he doesn't spew it, either. And he's a goddamn genius with an engine.

The project I'm finishing up for the shop today is a restoration of a beautiful old classic bike: a 1946 Harley Davidson WL. The guy who brought it in is some rich dude, a dentist or something who I guess found the bike in his grandfather's barn after he passed. The dentist is a weekend warrior, which we get a lot of in the shop, but the money people like him are willing to pay is really good. This bike has been a fucking joy to work on, except for one thing: the dentist guy specified that he wanted a non-original two-tone paint job on the restored bike. I tried to argue against it, and even tried to tell Hawk I wouldn't do it. But in the shop, Hawk's the boss, so I'm gritting my teeth and getting it done.

I work by myself for about an hour. The detailed work of the paint job focuses me enough that I have to devote most of my concentration to it and stop thinking about Sydney for a while. At one point, I hear Hawk on the phone in the office, and then he comes ambling out to me and takes a seat on an overturned five-gallon bucket.

"Rick Pierce is coming for the bike tomorrow," Hawk tells me, referring to the weekend warrior dentist.

"I'll have this done by lunchtime," I reply.

Hawk nods. "Looks good."

I snort. "Thanks." He knows I'm not a fan of the two-tone.

The small side door to the shop opens and Gunner comes striding in. "Hey, brothers," he announces to the large space. Murmurs of greeting come from the other side of the garage, where Striker and Thorn are working on a '66 Chevelle.

"Is *everybody* gonna be late today?" Hawk complains, glancing up at the clock on the wall.

"Relax, boss," Gunner grins at him. "Hey, Brick."

I lift my head up and nod at him. "Gun."

"You guys hear what happened at Ace Liquors?"

Hawk frowns. "No. What?"

"Got robbed overnight," he says. "They grabbed the guy who was closing up, took all the cash from the till and the safe. Beat the guy unconscious after he opened the safe for them. Took a bunch of liquor, smashed up whatever they couldn't carry with them, and left. Guy's in the hospital now. Beat up pretty bad, but I guess he's stable."

"Fuck," Hawk spits out. He stands up and lights a smoke. "Second one this month. The victim get a good look at any of them?"

"I guess they were wearing masks," Gunner replies, his expression turning dark. "He said he might have recognized one of their voices, but he wasn't sure."

"Fuck me running." I shake my head. "This isn't good."

There's been a rash of break-ins at local Tanner Springs businesses in the past few months. Most of them, like this one, seem motivated by the desire to get cash and then destroy shit for good measure — calculated to provoke maximum damage and outrage. This one's new in that they actually hurt someone. The local paper, the Tanner Springs Star, has been running increasingly hysterical stories about the crime wave, as well as a raft of letters to the editor demanding answers and justice for the people who've been victims. When I go into a restaurant or a gas station these days, more often than not it's what people are talking about.

More than one of the letters to the editor has implied it has something to do with the Lords of Carnage MC.

"Goddamnit," Hawk snarls. "One more excuse for Holloway and his men to keep us in their crosshairs."

"Yeah," I agree. "And you know what that means. We're likely to have another visit from the TSPD."

Jarred Holloway is the mayor of Tanner Springs. He's a smug, devious piece of shit who's had our club in his sights ever since he got elected a year and a half ago. He got elected on a "clean up Tanner Springs" platform, talking up a mostly nonexistent crime problem — and implying that the Lords of

Carnage was a bad element in town that needed to be ripped out at the roots.

I'm not gonna lie and say that the Lords haven't done our fair share of business that sat firmly on the wrong side of the law. But we've never been stupid enough to conduct those deals inside the city limits. Not to mention, we got our asses out of that shit and went legit right around the time Holloway took office. That was partly coincidence, and partly because we could see the writing on the wall. We knew Holloway was about to make our lives one hell of a lot harder in his quest to prove to Tanner Springs that he was tough on crime.

The building we're standing in right now used to be a warehouse we ran guns out of, among other things. We sold our last shipment off to the Death Devils, another club to the east of us, and made the space into a custom motorcycle and car shop instead. It's been a good source of income for us so far — not nearly as much as gun running, but safer and steadier. And ironically, since we opened the garage, Holloway's cops have come in and searched the place twice, looking for contraband. The last time they came in was right around the time the current "crime wave" started.

The fucked up thing is, none of these crimes started happening until *after* Jarred Holloway got elected. Funny, though, how the people who voted for him haven't seemed to notice that. All they see is that crime is on the rise. And for some reason, they believe he's the one who can stop it. And he's determined to make himself look like a goddamn hero to them. Probably at our expense.

6
BRICK

Sure enough, a few hours later -- right after lunch -- two cars pull up in the front lot of the garage. One's a late model white BMW 6 Series. The other sports the Tanner Springs PD logo on the side.

The driver's side door opens on the BMW, and out slides Mayor Jarred Holloway himself, looking especially douchey and sure of himself. His black hair is cut short and conservative, with a deep side part so straight it looks like he did it with a ruler. He's wearing a pale blue shirt that's starched within an inch of its damn life, and some light tan khakis with creases sharp enough to give him a paper cut. I consider coming up and giving him a pat on the back with my paint and oil stained hands. But then I'd have to touch the fucker.

The guy who gets out of the cop car turns out to be Brandt Crup, the new police chief, specially picked by Holloway to be his lackey.

"Oh, for feck's sake," mutters Thorn in disgust as we watch them approach. "I could've gone all day without seein' that wanker."

"Here we go," Gunner says, not moving from his spot leaning against the side of the building. The three of us are out here having a smoke. We don't move to greet them. Let those fuckers come to us.

"Hello there," Holloway calls as they saunter up, wearing his habitual shit-eating politician's grin.

Thorn gives me a look but says nothing.

"Mayor," I reply drily.

"We're looking to have a few words with your president," Crup announces officiously. He's pudgy and soft, with a receding hairline that makes his forehead look enormous. The buttons on his shirt are pulling slightly.

"Is that so?" Thorn asks. "And here we thought you were just coming for a friendly chin wag."

"Is Rock around?" Holloway asks, still with that artificial smile.

"He's inside."

Crup takes a step forward but Thorn stops him.

"You wait right here, now, gentlemen," he says in a tone that's friendly to the point of mockery. "He'll be right out in a jif." He turns on his heel and heads into the garage. Gunner and I continue to take drags on our cigarettes, not bothering to make small talk. The four of us stand in silence. Holloway's smile falters only a little, and then he pastes it back on, trying his best to look completely unfazed. Crup sneers and blows out a dry laugh.

A minute or so later, Thorn returns with Rock. Hawk is with them.

"Holloway," Rock says by way of greeting. His voice is completely devoid of any expression.

"Rock Anthony," Holloway nods, showing his teeth. "I remember speaking to you at the town fundraiser for the library a while back."

"Glad to know I'm so memorable," Rock replies.

"I don't suppose you've heard about the break-in at Ace Liquors last night," Chief Crup interjects. He squints his eyes and scans all of us in turn, like he's looking for someone to crack.

"Matter of fact, we did," Hawk replies. "Shame."

"You boys happen to know anything about that?" Crup continues.

Hawk instantly bristles at being called a boy, but you'd have to know him pretty well to see it. A muscle tightens in his jaw. "Heard the news through the grapevine. You catch anyone yet?"

"Not yet," Crup drawls. "But seems to me, there's not that many 'elements' in town that are likely to be breaking into local businesses, looking for money."

"Probably not," Rock nods. "Should make it easier for you to find them, then."

"Uh-huh." Crup nods toward the inside of the garage. "You think if we went in there and looked around, we'd find anything to help us figure out who the perps are?"

"Can't imagine how," Gunner says evenly. "Maybe your time would be better spent looking around at the actual crime scene."

Crup snorts. "Funny. You're a funny guy."

"That's what I've been told," Gunner grins.

But Rock's starting to show some anger. "You got something to say, you say it."

"I'm saying the Lords of Carnage seem like they're doing pretty well these days," Crup says, nodding toward the garage. "Lots of money seems to be flowing into the club."

"Yeah. Lots of *legit* money," I counter.

"That right?" Crup retorts, turning to me. "You think if we got a search warrant and took a little look inside, we'd see how *legit* you are?"

"Oh, fer Chrissake, do we look like the kind of petty goddamn thugs who would knock over a fecking liquor store?" Thorn spits out, finally losing patience. "Christ, why don't you go look for some tweakers or something? That's who most likely has been doing this shite. For quick drug money."

"That so?" Crup narrows his eyes at Thorn.

"Look, Holloway," Rock cuts them off and addresses the mayor. "You're barking up the wrong tree. And what's more, I think you know it."

"Oh, I'm not so sure," Holloway says mildly.

Crup raises an angry finger and points it at Rock. "You've been warned. You're on notice," he hisses, like he's in some kind of movie.

Beside me, Gunner bursts out laughing.

The mayor flicks an annoyed glance at Crup, and then turns his gaze on us, one by one. "Well, you *boys* keep your noses clean," he says in a cheerful tone, "and I'm sure you won't have any problems. The people of Tanner Springs deserve to live in a town they feel safe in. It's my job to make sure they do." He nods at Rock and gives us his best campaign-poster smile. "You all have a good day, now."

Holloway turns on his heels and heads back to his car. Crup follows close behind.

"Christ, I'd love to throttle the both of 'em," Thorn murmurs.

"Cheer up," I mutter. "Crup looks a little wet behind the ears to be a police chief. Maybe we'll get lucky and he'll shoot himself while he's cleaning his gun."

"You think they actually think we have anything to do with this shit?" Hawk asks Rock as we watch them drive away.

"Maybe Crup does," Rock answers. "He's a fucking idiot. But I think Holloway knows this is bullshit. He's politicking."

Rock decides to head back to the clubhouse to talk to our VP, Angel. The rest of us head inside and get back to work, but Chief Crup's little visit has cast a pall over the day. By the time five o'clock rolls around, everyone's more than a little out of sorts. Me included.

"That's it," Hawk finally says, slamming the hood of the Chevelle. "I need a fucking drink."

"Hallelujah," Gunner agrees. "You coming to the clubhouse?" he asks, turning toward me.

"You bet." I grab a rag to wipe off my hands. "I'll catch up with you, just as soon as I get some of this paint off."

I go clean myself up and then head out to my bike. The late afternoon air is warm and smells like cut grass, which is a welcome change from paint fumes in the shop. As I pass through downtown, I slow the bike just slightly as I near the

Golden Cup. I glance in, and manage to catch a glimpse of long red hair through the window before I throttle up and continue toward the clubhouse.

7
SYDNEY

The next day, even though I hate to admit it to myself, I'm sort of hoping that Gavin will come into the coffee shop. But the morning comes and goes, and he doesn't make an appearance. It's a Saturday, though, and I have to remind myself I've never seen him come in on a weekend.

Hailey arrives in the early afternoon to do a short shift so I can take care of some paperwork. There's a lull between customers when she gets here, so I have a chance to chat with her before I go back to my office.

"How was your meeting after school yesterday?" I'm asking her. "I never thought to ask you yesterday afternoon." I'd remembered the math test, but not that.

"The Senior Activities Committee? It was okay." She lifts one shoulder in a half-shrug. "There were a lot of super-popular kids that showed up for it — not really my scene, usually. But I guess I'll keep going to it for now."

"What does this committee do, exactly?" I reach under the counter for a stack of to-go cups and set them next to the register.

She gives me little sarcastic smirk. "Well, we basically organize activities for the seniors."

I snort. "Right. I got that. Like what?"

"Like…" she starts counting on her fingers. "There's painting the senior wall. And the senior boys' party, and the senior girls' party. And a bunch of dances. And the senior float for the homecoming parade. And the all night party, and senior skip day."

"Wow. Are you going to have any time to actually study and learn things, in between all the parties?"

"Seriously?" She eyes me. "You sound like a mom."

God. I kind of do, I realize. "Sorry. But it does seem like that's an awful lot of stuff cutting into time that you might need to do… oh, I don't know… *homework,* and things like that."

Hailey flips a dismissive hand at me. "Please. Tanner Springs High is *such* a sluff school. I only brought books home like, three times last year. I get all my homework done in my study hall. Don't worry about me."

"Okay, then, I'll worry about *me*," I grin. "Are you going to have time to work here at the shop, with all your extra-curricular activities?"

"Well, actually…" she bites her lip. "I *was* going to talk to you about that." She frowns apologetically. "Do you think there's any way we could switch my schedule around so I could work evenings instead of after school sometimes? We have to sign up for the stuff we're going to help with on the committee. If I had at least a couple of days a week where I knew I didn't have to be here until later, I could sign up for more stuff."

"For someone who isn't really into that 'scene,' you really seem to be throwing yourself into this," I tease her.

"Well…" she says slyly, "There *is* a guy I'm kind of crushing on who's on the committee, too."

"Aha! There it is!" I crow. "So your friend Melissa isn't *really* the reason you joined."

"No, she is," Hailey protests. Her face turns an adorable shade of pink. "But… when I got to the meeting, Teddy just happened to be there, too."

I'm about to start grilling Hailey on every detail of her crush, when a crisply dressed older lady comes into the shop. Her silver-white hair is short and coiffed into an attractive bob, and she's wearing surprisingly fashionable round tortoise-shell glasses. I've seen her in here once or twice before. She always comes in by herself, and she's always carrying a thick paperback with her to read while she drinks her coffee.

"Hello there," I greet her. "What can I get you?"

She smiles distractedly at me. "I'll take a medium, non-fat, no foam, extra shot, half-caf vanilla latte. For here."

"Sure thing." I ring her up. "Have a seat, and I'll bring your drink out to you in just a minute."

Hailey raises her eyes at me as she wanders off to find a table. "Wow. She's really embraced the specialty coffee culture."

I make the woman's drink, and just as I'm finishing up, my phone buzzes in my pocket. I have Hailey bring the latte out to her and check my messages.

It's a text from a number I was hoping I'd never have to see again.

Thought I wouldnt find u didnt u bitch? Wheres my fucking money?

A little shiver of dread ripples through me. *He's found me.*

I always knew it could happen, though I was hoping against hope it wouldn't.

Does he know where I am? Does he know where I live? Does he know anything more than my number?

I stand frozen to the spot, trying not to panic. Of course I knew Devon would be able to find me if he wanted to. It's not easy to disappear these days, since everyone has an electronic footprint that's hard to erase. There are so many things I could have done to hide that I didn't do: change my name, leave the country… Instead, I chose to just leave Atlantic City, taking what I knew was mine, and refuse to live my life in fear.

I chose to believe I was small enough potatoes to Devon that he would leave me alone. That he'd decide tracking me down wasn't worth the trouble.

Looks like I may have chosen wrong.

My fingers hover above the screen as I try to decide what to do. Responding to his text would be crazy, but not responding isn't going to fool him. If he has this number, he *knows* it's me.

That money was me taking back what was mine, I tell myself fiercely. *It was money he stole from me in the first place. However he wants to spin it in his head, that's the truth. And we both know it.*

"So, is it okay?"

Hailey startles me out of my thoughts.

"It what okay?" I stammer.

"Changing me to evenings sometimes."

"Oh." I mentally shake my head to clear it. "Um, sure, I think so. Let me take a look at the schedule. I'll just have to teach you how to close by yourself." I shove my phone back in my pocket and give her what I hope is a normal smile.

"Awesome," she grins. "You're so cool."

"Hailey," I say in a bright voice, hoping she can't hear how it's shaking. "I have to go run a quick errand. Can you take over for a while until I get back?"

"Sure, no prob," she nods. "I've got it covered."

"Thanks. I'll be back in an hour or so." I walk a little unsteadily down the hallway, but instead of turning in to my office, I keep going, out the back door to my car. With a hand that's started to shake, I toss the phone down on the ground directly behind one of the rear tires.

Then, I get in, turn the key in the ignition, throw the car into reverse, and deliberately back over it.

And then, I head across town to my cellular provider. To get a new cell phone, and a new number.

8

SYDNEY

I'm not running away from anybody. So what if he found me? I'm not hiding from anything.

An hour and a half later, I'm back at the coffee shop, trying as hard as I can to concentrate on my paperwork and casting furtive glances at my new phone, even though Devon can't possibly have the new number yet.

I have *got* to put this out of my mind. I can't let him get into my head like this. He doesn't have the right. *He can't control me. I'm stronger than that.*

Devon was always an aggressive player. He always had an attitude, and took losing more personally than a professional should. I knew instinctively that he would take my leaving as a loss, a blow to his ego. Still, he's practical, too, to the point of being cynical. I was only one of the players in his stable. He had plenty more when I was there, and plenty of bigger, more reliable earners than me.

The fact that he was also romantically interested in me, though, changes the equation. I have to consider the possibility that his ego might have overridden his practical side where I'm concerned.

As I get online and place some orders for supplies, I think about what my dad used to say about bluffing in cards. Poker was never my game, but Dad started out his career as a professional poker player. Some people never bluff, or almost never. Others are habitual bluffers. The best bluffers don't get emotionally invested in their bluffing, one way or another. The worst ones are the ones who get off on it — who get off on the idea of pulling one over on someone else.

I have to make myself assume that Devon is bluffing. Getting off on the idea of making me scared. If that's what he's doing, then probably the best thing I can do is not call his bluff. Let him think I'm afraid. Let him think that he's won, and cross my fingers that it will be enough.

* * *

"Okay," I tell Hailey when I go back out to the front of the shop. "I think I've figured out a schedule for you to start working nights and closing for me a few times a week. But in exchange, you have to tell me more about Teddy."

Hailey is only too happy to comply. I listen with half an ear as she chats happily about her crush, whom she describes as kind of geeky but, in her words, "stealth hot." Apparently,

Hailey's friend Melissa is convinced that Teddy was stealing glances at her all during the meeting yesterday. It's super cute to see Hailey so happy and hopeful, flushed with excitement, in the beginning stages of something that might turn out to be a major romance or might just be a tiny blip on the screen of her young life.

A strange, heavy feeling seems to take over my limbs as I look around the shop and listen to Hailey's voice rise and fall with teenage inflections. The scene in front of me right now is so reassuringly *normal.* Almost impossibly so. Tanner Springs seems — to me, anyway — like some All-American small town that someone invented in the pages of a book, or on a movie set. Hailey's just a normal high school student, doing normal, high school things. Her life is just that... so *normal.* And so very different from the one I was living at her age.

I feel a pang of regret, which I quickly push down. *Can't change the past,* I tell myself. And I know that's true. But it doesn't stop me from wishing I could, sometimes.

I do remember being Hailey's age, though. As different from hers as my life was, I remember how incredibly important and earth-shattering the smallest things could feel. I remember how important my first kiss felt. How transcendent a first love can feel. How brutal a first rejection can be.

And yet, looking back, so much of what seemed like pinnacles of my existence at the time are moments I can barely even remember now. So many things that I thought were almost literally the end of the world were nothing, compared to the private disasters that just snuck up to me later, taking me completely by surprise.

My chest tightens a little as I find myself wondering whether Hailey will ever have someone hurt her. *Really* hurt her. Whether she'll be in a relationship someday and realize that the man she's with is no good — that she's stayed far too long in something she never should have started in the first place.

That she'll have to walk, or run, away from a relationship, and leave a little chunk of herself behind in order to save what she has left.

Another customer has come into the shop. It's a girl of high school age, and it's clear that Hailey knows her from the way she jumps up and bounces over to the counter to serve her. A few seconds later, four more kids about the same age trail in behind the first one. They all order elaborate, sugary drinks with mountains of whipped cream and large, calorie-laden pastries. I quietly marvel at them all — on the cusp of adulthood, play-acting at being grown-ups with budding caffeine habits.

God, I feel old.

I let Hailey serve her friends, bubbling with laughter and gossip, and move off to the far end of the counter to uselessly check my new phone, with my new number, for messages.

"Excuse me, dear."

I look up to see the older lady in the tortoise-shell frames. She's holding her empty cup in one hand, and her book in the other. She's been here for more than two hours, I realize. She must be almost finished reading it by now.

"I'd like another latte, if you don't mind. I was wondering if you could make it for me, so I wouldn't have to wait for these young people." She nods at the cluster of Hailey's friends at the counter.

"Oh! Yes, of course." I shove my phone in my pocket and take her cup from her. "I'll give you a fresh cup, though. Can you remind me exactly what your order was?"

"A medium, non-fat, no foam, extra shot, half-caf vanilla latte," she recites.

"Got it." I start making her drink. "Are you enjoying your book?" I ask, to make conversation.

"Oh. Yes." She looks down, as though embarrassed. "It's a wonderful new addiction I've discovered since you opened your shop: Sitting down to read a book with a delicious cup of coffee."

"I agree," I grin at her. "It's one of my favorite things to do. It might be one of the main reasons I opened the Golden Cup in the first place."

"A fellow reader! That's lovely." Her friendly smile changes to a dismayed frown. "Oh, but you never get to enjoy you own shop, since you're always working!"

"Well, I *do* get to enjoy watching others do it." I pour skim milk into the steamer. "That's a nice vicarious pleasure."

"Yes, I suppose that's true."

"What are you reading, if you don't mind me asking?"

She purses her lips, clearly a bit embarrassed. "Oh, I have a weakness for regency romances." She holds up her book so I can see the cover. It features a pale woman with an empire-waist dress and an elaborate hairstyle. "True escapism," she admits. "But I do love them."

For a moment, neither of us speaks, the whoosh of steaming milk too loud to call over. When I'm finished, I grab a saucer and set it down on the counter, then place the cup on top.

"There you are," I tell her. "Enjoy."

"Thank you. By the way, my name is Beverly."

"I'm Sydney," I smile at her.

"Sydney." She gives a slight nod of her head. "That's an unusual name."

"It's actually my middle name," I say, not sure why I'm telling her this. "My first name is Violet."

"Well!" she beams. "Violet is my sister's name!" She seems so pleased at this connection that it's infectious.

"That is a coincidence!" I grin. "Older or younger?"

"Younger, by three years. She lives in Nogales, Arizona, with her husband now." She hesitates for just a second. "I hope it's not rude, but out of curiosity, may I ask why you go by your middle name?"

"Violet was my mom's idea," I tell her. "My dad didn't like the name. They split up when I was young, and my dad ended up raising me. So, now I'm Sydney. Syd, to him."

"Oh." Beverly coughs and glances away, clearly embarrassed. She needn't be, though. I don't remember my mom, so her absence in my life isn't something I really notice much.

I do miss my father, though. He's been gone for more than seven years now. His face comes to me now — his familiar, roguish smile — and a familiar wave of grief rolls through me.

"Sydney!" Hailey comes up to me breathlessly, interrupting our conversation. "That's him!"

"That's who?" I frown.

"Teddy!" she stage whispers, and tilts her head toward the large table in the center of the room where her high school friends are sitting.

56

"Which one?" I cut my eyes toward them.

"The tall, geeky one with the dark hair." Hailey is muttering while trying not to move her lips. I'd burst out laughing if she didn't look so earnest.

I move my head slightly and take a quick look at the gangly boy talking animatedly with his friends. Teddy is the kind of boy who still looks like he's growing into his limbs. Beyond the gawkiness though, he's definitely cute — the kind of kid I probably would have had a crush on myself at that age.

"He's cute," I acknowledge, shooting Hailey a quick nod, then turn pointedly to Beverly. "Hailey, I was just helping Beverly here. Beverly, this is Hailey. She works for me after school and on weekends."

"Nice to meet you, Hailey," Beverly says, extending a hand.

Hailey's face turns sheepish as she shakes it. "Nice to meet you, too. Sorry I interrupted you."

Beverly gives her an amused smile. "No need to apologize. I was young once, too."

She bends to pick up her latte. Balancing it carefully on top of her book, she goes back to her table, and Hailey goes back to surreptitiously spying on Teddy.

I'm left alone with my persistently maudlin thoughts — to imagine Hailey as an old woman, and Beverly as a young girl. Both of them bookends, at the dawn and dusk of what they hope will be a journey that ends with that rarest of gifts.

A real love. A soulmate. A fairy tale come true.

9
BRICK

"So, what are we gonna do about this shit?"

At the head of the table, Rock is looking tired. Next to him, Angel, our VP, wears a deep frown of concentration. The mood at church this morning is somber and tense. We just heard that last night, there was a fire at one of the businesses downtown. The whole place was gutted, and the police are already talking arson.

"I dunno, but people are getting damn nervous around town." Gunner leans back in his chair. "You know this fire's going to be on the front page of the paper next week."

"Yeah," Angel says in disgust. "With all sorts of leading language about criminals 'hiding in plain sight' and shit like that."

"It's only a matter of time before they start naming us directly," I mutter.

Hawk clears his throat. "You know," he begins, "I think we're gonna have to consider the possibility that the cops know it's not us. Or even that they're working with Holloway to pin it on us somehow."

"I have considered that," Rock barks. "Question is, what the fuck do we do about it?"

"Maybe we have to find out who it is ourselves," I say. "Doesn't seem like the PD is doing much about it, other than swaggering around town and giving quotes to the Tanner Springs Star."

"That means a hell of a lot of man-hours doing shit the cops should be doing," Rock retorts.

"Yeah. I know." I look around the table. "It'll definitely put a burden on us. And we don't really have enough men to do it."

"That's the truth of it," Thorn nods. "Even with the prospects."

"Maybe it's time to start thinking about accepting some new blood," Geno, our Treasurer, rumbles.

Striker speaks up. "I been thinking that, too. For more reasons than one. Shit, the Iron Spiders have been growing their ranks damn quickly lately, by the looks of it. We can't afford to let them get too much bigger than us if we want to hold on to our territory."

The Iron Spiders are a club to the south of us. We've been involved in a war with them off and on for the last year or so. It's no secret they've been trying to weaken our club, and come after our territory. So far we've managed to avoid any fatalities on our side, but it's been close. The last time they came after us, Hawk's old lady Samantha got caught in the middle and almost got killed.

Angel nods his agreement. "We don't have any way of knowing exactly how many men the Spiders have, but if I had to guess, I'd say they might be closing in on almost twice as many patched members as we do by now." He doesn't say any more, and he doesn't have to. We've held our own — better than held our own — against them, but if their numbers are as big as he thinks they are, that won't be the case for much longer.

"There's also the possibility that the Spiders are behind all this shit going down in Tanner Springs," I reply. "Could be a back-door way of fucking with us. Weakening our hold on our territory."

"That's true," Tweak murmurs. "Keeping us busy by siccing the law on us."

There's silence for a few moments. I expect Rock to say something, but he doesn't do anything but stare murderously at the table.

"How many of you know men you think would be a good fit to be a Lord of Carnage?" Angel eventually asks, looking around. Almost a dozen hands go up. He nods. "Good.

Look, I think we need to move quickly here. Let's actively recruit some prospects, some men we think are top notch. All of you try to think of at least one person you can vouch for. But no wet behind the ears kids. We need numbers, but numbers aren't enough. And I think we need to look at moving forward with patching in the prospects we do have, if we think they're ready."

"I think Bullet and Lug Nut are ready," Geno offers, talking about our latest prospects. "They're tough, and steady in a crisis. I think they've proven themselves."

"Yeah. And Bullet's the only prospect I've ever seen who can drink me under the table," Gunner smirks. A chorus of loud laughs goes around the table. It's a welcome moment of levity.

"You think we should put them up for a vote?" Angel asks, turning to Rock.

"Oh? My opinion is requested?" Rock sneers back.

Angel eyes him levelly. "I'm asking a question."

For a second, it feels like the tension in the air just before a lightning strike.

No one speaks. Rock looks like he's waiting for Angel to say more, but Angel doesn't take the bait.

Finally, Rock turns away and looks at all of us. "We put Bullet and Lug up for a vote, next church. But that doesn't solve our problem. New prospects take time to vet. Meantime, we need to act."

"We ought to be talking to some of the local business owners," I suggest. "The ones who've already been hit, to begin with. Ask them if they noticed any unusual activity or anything before the break-in. Offer our help."

"Good idea," Gunner nods. "We should think about what all the places that have already been hit have in common. Try to figure out what the motives are. Might help us get an idea of which businesses might be next."

"Yeah," Hawk agrees. "And it'll be good PR for us. Slow people down from assuming it's us if they see us trying to help deal with the problem."

"One more thing," Angel muses, turning to Rock. "I think maybe we should talk to the Death Devils." The Devils are a club to the east of us. Our two clubs have done business in the past, and we've been making moves toward a tentative alliance with them. "I think it'd be a good idea to ask them whether they've been seeing anything similar where they are. Get their take on what the Spiders are up to. Maybe we can figure out a deal to work together on this. At least until our numbers are up."

Rock grudgingly nods. "That's a good idea. I'll get in touch with Oz. See what he has to say. If he's willing to do a meet-up."

We talk for a few more minutes about who's gonna approach which businesses and report back, and then Rock adjourns the meeting. The brothers all file out of the chapel, except for Angel and Rock, who close the door behind us.

"Fuck," Gunner mutters to me as we walk over and signal to Jewel, our main bartender, for a beer. "I don't like whatever it is that's going on between Rock and Angel. Last thing the club needs right now is the two of them going at each other."

Jewel eyes us for a second as we pull up stools at the bar, but she knows better than to ask anything. Silently, she pops the top off a couple of bottles for us and moves discreetly down to the other end.

"No shit, brother." I take a long pull of the icy liquid. "Fuck, that tastes good. Whatever it is, though, it's between them."

"Yeah," Gunner glowers. "I sure as shit hope they figure it out."

We nurse our beers for a few minutes and try to talk about something else. Eventually, I finish mine and stand up. "I think I'm gonna head home for a while," I tell him.

"You coming back to the clubhouse later?"

"Yeah, maybe," I say noncommittally. "I'll catch up with you later, all right?"

"Sure thing, brother. See you when I see you."

I lift a finger goodbye, and walk outside to my bike, exhaling a little as the tension leaves my shoulders. Normally, I'd hang out here with the rest of the brothers, and maybe grab one of the apartments upstairs to sleep here tonight.

But right now, I'm looking for a little time to myself. To sort through all the shit that's in my head.

10
BRICK

An hour later, I'm back at my house, staring at the lake with a cold one in my hand. The sun is just starting its descent toward the horizon. I've watched its path at least a hundred times out here, just like this, by myself.

I came back to the lake after church because I needed some time to relax, and to think. Everything that's been going on the last couple of days is whirring around in my brain, and sometimes I just need some goddamn silence to sort it all out. That's why I bought this place. Such as it is.

In the little more than a year I've lived here, I've basically rebuilt what was a falling down shack from the ground up. The house wasn't worth much when I bought it, so what I'd saved up after eight years in the Marines was just about enough to pay for the whole thing in cash. Even so, this place is my goddamn pride and joy. It's funny, but even after a full day of working at the garage, a lot of times the thing I look most forward to when I get back home is firing up the bandsaw or ripping out some old wiring. It's therapeutic somehow, taking something that's run down and fucked up, and making it strong and solid again. That's one of the reasons I like working at the garage restoring bikes and cars, too. But here at the house, the results of my work are mine, and mine alone.

Before this house, I'd never really had much before that I could call mine. In my childhood, I went from being a burden and an afterthought to my parents, to being passed around from foster home to foster home by people who made it clear to me I wasn't part of their family and never would be. I joined the Marines as soon as I turned eighteen, and spent the next eight years of my life working hard and playing harder, with nothing to go back home for during my leaves, and no goals except doing the job I was sent with my regiment to do.

When I got out of the Marines, I was rootless, and aimless. I had no idea where I was gonna go when I got back home to the States, and no fucking clue what I was gonna do with myself. All I knew was that I didn't want to make a career out of being in the Corps. I chafed a lot at the rules and the hierarchy inherent in military service. Even though I rose up fairly quickly in the ranks, the structure didn't always sit well with me, especially whenever I saw dumb shits with higher ranks lording it over men who were the real backbone of the unit. The camaraderie, though, and the pure physicality of it — those things I liked.

That's probably what ended up drawing me into the Lords of Carnage, after I got out. Gunner and I had served together in the same platoon, and he knew I was having a tough time finding my way out in the civilian world, much as I'd thought I wanted it. He was the one who gave me a call and told me to ride out here to Tanner Springs. Told me he had something to talk over with me. Something he thought would be a good fit.

Now, a handful of years later, here I am. Turns out Gunner was right. He sponsored me to get patched into the Lords of Carnage, the club he'd always thought of joining someday. Now, instead of a Staff Sergeant or a Master Sergeant, I'm the club's Enforcer. Instead of enforcing rules by military procedures, I do it with my fists. And weapons.

It's a much better fit. For the most part.

Now, for the first time, I have a family. A real one. Brothers who have my back. A place of my own, where I can lock the goddamn door at night and be left the hell alone. Most of all, silence. And peace. It's lonely sometimes, but it's mine.

Absently, I pull a cigarette from the pack and light it, sitting back in the Adirondack chair I pulled from a dumpster and refurbished. Taking a deep drag, I let it out with a heavy, troubled sigh.

Church today has left me on edge. Not because of anything that was decided. Not because of this bullshit crime wave in Tanner Springs. Not even because of the threat on the horizon posed by a growing Iron Spiders club, and what that means for the ongoing war between us.

I'm on edge because I'm starting to have serious doubts about my club president.

An Enforcer, above all, has to be very loyal to the man who is his president. Sometimes I'm a bodyguard. Sometimes I'm sent out to do the more violent tasks that need to be done: a hit, or a beatdown, or even ending someone, if that's what's called for. I'm the president's arm of justice. I do what he tells me.

One of my jobs is to keep the other brothers in check if need be. Not only when we're out on a run or in a situation of danger, but also within the club itself. I have to be able to carry out the president's orders without question — even and especially if that means I have to face off against one of my own brothers to do it. Insubordination, just like in the military, is not an option.

But unlike in the military, I've never had cause to question the judgment of the man whose orders I'm bound to execute in the Lords of Carnage.

Until now.

It's nothing specific. Nothing I can quite put my finger on.

But for a while now, I'm not really sure where Rock Anthony's head is at. I think some of the other brothers are feeling it, too. I see the way they look from Rock to Angel. They're wondering where the club's heading. If there's a crisis in the making.

And that makes me nervous. Because I've never been much good at enforcing rules I don't believe in.

Eventually, my cigarette runs down to ash, my beer is empty, and my ass is starting to get sore. With a sigh, I haul myself up and stretch my arms over my head. Enough thinking for now. There's a bathroom renovation inside waiting for me. And God knows laying shower tile is a fuck of a lot simpler than contemplating the future of a club that I've grown to love, but don't know quite how to enforce anymore.

11
SYDNEY

"…So, then, you wrap up the rest of the pastries individually and put them in the day-old discount basket for the next day," I'm telling Hailey as we walk through the shop. "After that, clean out the pastry case, sanitize all the trays, and set up the case for the morning. Then, you clean the espresso machine and run the cleaning cycle."

I've sat down and made a list of all the things I do when I close, to make it easier on Hailey when she starts doing it herself. I point to it from time to time as I talk, to show her that everything is on the list, so she doesn't have to remember it all. She's listening attentively — so much so that it's actually really cute to see how earnest she is. I'm glad, too, because this stuff is important. If she doesn't take it seriously, customers might get a mouthful of rancid cream, or sit down at a sticky table first thing in the morning. I want everything to be perfect at the Golden Cup, so every person that comes in here for the first time wants to come back again.

"You need to clean and sanitize the coffee urns, too, and all the bar tools. The pitchers, spoons, containers — everything," I continue. "Wipe off all the exteriors, too, and make everything look as clean as possible. Then, when you're satisfied with all that, mop the floor, wipe off the tables and chairs, and look around for anything else that needs to be cleaned. Oh, and don't forget the bathroom. Then restock the lids and cups and the condiment bar — minus the milk and cream, of course. Then, take out the trash on your way out, and you're done."

Hailey blows out a breath. "Good thing you wrote all this down. It's a lot to remember."

"Don't worry," I reassure her. "I'll come in and help you close the first couple of times, so you can ask any questions that come up then."

"Thanks for letting me do this," she says sincerely. "I know it means adjusting your schedule to fit mine. You didn't have to, I know."

"Honestly, it's kind of nice." I smile. "After all, this way I actually get some evenings free once in a while. Hell, I might even end up with a social life, if I'm not careful."

"What do I do with the cash in the till?" Hailey asks, glancing toward the cash register.

"Oh, yeah. That's another thing. You're going to have to balance the cash register drawer every night." I frown. "Let's save that for another time, though. After you're feeling confident about the other stuff. For now, you'll just put the cash drawer in the safe. I'll have taken out most of the money myself, so there will only be a couple hundred dollars in it."

"Okay, good," she laughs. "Because my brain is starting to feel like it's going to explode."

I set Hailey to work cleaning and wiping down things, and I grab the till and go in the back to count the cash drawer. I'm used to doing all of this stuff by myself every night, and it's really, *really* nice to have someone help me for once. At this rate, I'll get out of here in half the time it usually takes me. *Luxury!* Already, I'm dreaming of drawing a hot bath and pouring myself a glass of chilled white wine. It's the little things, after all.

A loud pounding shakes me out of my little fantasy. A moment later, Hailey's voice comes wafting toward me from the front.

"Hey, um… Sydney?"

"Yeah!" I'm just shutting the door to the safe.

"There's someone at the front door!"

"Just tell them we're closed!" I get someone at least once a week who raps on the door to be let in, even though the door's locked and the hours are clearly posted right there.

"Sydney? I think maybe you should do it."

"Seriously?" I mutter to myself as I wipe my hands on my jeans and turn around. This is something Hailey is going to have to learn to deal with if she's going to be closing by herself. Already thinking about the talking-to I'm going to give her once I've dealt with this, I walk out into the shop and prepare myself to be polite but firm to the customer.

"Hailey, you're going to have to..." I begin, but when my eyes land on the face peering at me from the other side of the glass, I trail off and go silent.

He's tall, and dark. His eyes feel like lasers on mine in their intensity.

My skin feels all goose-bumpy, all of a sudden.

I glance quickly over at Hailey, who's looking at me with a wide-eyed *"I told you so!"* expression.

I should just yell through the door that we're closed. But something in his face tells me he's not here to fill his to-go cup.

Uncertainly, I flip the lock and open the door a crack. "Hi."

"Hey," he rumbles.

God, his voice is like velvet. I suppress a shiver.

"Uh, we're closed." My voice comes out weirdly breathy.

"I know." He nods once. "Look, can I talk to you?" He glances over at Hailey. "It's work related."

I can't *imagine* what this is about. What the hell does 'work related' mean? Is he here to bitch at me *again* about the whole nitrous oxide debacle? That seems too weird, though, even for him.

I can't believe what I'm about to do, but curiosity gets the better of me.

So I pull open the door and let him in.

When I turn back toward the counter, Hailey is openly *staring*. I suppress an eye-roll, knowing that she's going to make a *huge* deal out of this when she comes into work tomorrow.

"Hailey, this is… Brick," I say, because that's what polite people do.

"Hi." She's standing there frozen to the spot, almost like she's been frozen in a game of freeze tag. I have *never* seen Hailey act so suddenly shy. She looks like a cornered rabbit.

"Nice to meet you," Gavin growls.

"Nicemeetyoutoo," she mumbles.

"Hailey, it looks like you're almost done there," I observe. "You can take off now. I'll come in early and finish up in the morning." I don't know what Gavin has to say to me, but I do know I definitely don't want to deal with Hailey hovering around, pretending not to listen but actually eavesdropping on every word. Especially because afterwards, I'll have to deal with a raft of questions from her, which I know I will *not* want to answer.

"Are you sure?" she asks uncertainly. "I mean, I only have the coffee urns to clean out, and then I'm done."

"Yeah, it's fine." I wave her off. "I can get that done tomorrow before I open up."

"Okay." She's clearly reluctant, but she pulls her apron over her head and loops it over the hook next to the back hallway. "I'll see you tomorrow after school, then."

"Sounds good."

She grabs her backpack from the cabinet where she always stashes it, and wanders slowly to the door. "Okay, bye, then," she murmurs, giving me an uncertain little wave. "Bye, uh, Brick."

Gavin lifts his chin at her. "Have a good one."

I wait until she's out the door, and watch her unlock her bike and ride away. Then I turn back toward Gavin, who's standing in the middle of the room. Looking hot. And bothered.

Like hot-sexy, not temperature-hot.

And bothered like kind of preoccupied. Not... you know... *hot and bothered.*

Good Lord. I'm blathering in my own head.

"Hey," he says again.

"You said that already."

"Yeah. I know."

"Oh."

Well.

This is…

Well… *awkward* would certainly be one way to describe it.

I haven't seen him since the day the nitrous oxide cartridge exploded. And I had sort of been hoping that the next time he came into the shop, I'd have a long line of customers to deal with so we wouldn't have to talk much.

I've never been the shy, retiring type. My dad made sure to raise me so I could hold my own from a young age. But there's something about this man that seems to reduce me to some sort of giggling schoolgirl. It's maddening. I'm worse than Hailey with her high school crush.

Not that I have a crush on him, of course.

Ugh.

I give my self a stern mental talking-to to get hold of my damn self, and motion for him to sit down at one of the tables. He flips the seat around so he can lean his forearms on the backrest. I take the other chair, moving it back just a hair before I sit down, to give me just a little more distance from him.

"So, uh, what did you need to talk to me about?" I ask, in my best *we totally didn't almost kiss a couple of days ago* voice.

He seems distracted, his face twisting into a displeased frown. "Is it usually just the two of you closing this place down for the day?"

"No. Normally, it's only one of us. Mainly me."

"What?"

"I was teaching Hailey to do it, so she could do it herself sometimes. That's why she was here tonight."

"Seriously?" His eyes grow wide and stormy. "You're usually here all alone, after dark?"

"Sorry. I had to let my security detail go," I say, a note of sarcasm in my voice. "They got too expensive." What the hell did he think I do? He's literally never seen any other employees in the shop, because I don't have any other employees except Hailey.

"That's crazy," he says with a dark look. "You're totally exposed here. The whole front of the store is plate-glass windows. Anyone out there can see everything you do."

I snort. "Yeah. It's totally scary that they can watch me wipe down counters and re-stock to-go cups."

"I'm fucking serious, Sydney," he says angrily.

My mind was a swirl of emotions when he showed up just now, but it's amazing how quickly they're settling back into just one: *irritation.* "Look," I scowl. "The door's locked the whole time." I nod toward the entryway. "And seeing through the windows goes both ways, you know. Anyone who wanted to jump me, I'd see them out there right away. I've got my cell phone," I say, patting my back pocket. "Hell, I've even got pepper spray on my keychain." I lean back and cross my arms. "I'd be in the back and have it out in seconds, even if they decided to bust down the door."

He doesn't say anything for a moment, but his brow furrows, so I can tell he doesn't like my rationale. I resist the urge to keep explaining myself — *after all, what business is it of his?* I think crossly. I'm done trying to justify myself. He can just leave if he doesn't like it.

"Do you have a security system?" he challenges.

"No. I don't." My tone is defiant. I'd thought about installing one when I first opened up, but honestly, it just seemed too expensive. I'm not about to tell him that, though.

"How often do you close this late?"

"It's not even that late," I protest. As soon as the words are out of my mouth, I'm pissed off at myself for even answering him. "Look, Gavin," in a tone that clearly says *I'm being patient but I don't need to keep listening to this.* "Am I to assume that you came here specifically to critique *my* decisions about how late to keep *my* coffee shop open?"

"Sydney," he says, his tone exasperated. "You're a woman alone, in plain sight of anyone driving by. You know you're a sitting duck, right?" He runs a rough hand through his hair. "Pepper spray or not. And by the way, pepper spray doesn't always work. It doesn't affect everyone. And if an intruder is high enough, or drunk enough, it probably won't do much."

"Look, what is this about?" I ask impatiently. "Are you trying to tell me you stopped by my shop after it was closed because you just suddenly got incredibly concerned for my welfare? I don't remember asking you to stop by and give me your thoughts on how to run my business." My voice is rising, but I don't care. "And besides, I'm not an idiot! And I would appreciate it if you'd stop treating me like one. I'm not *completely* helpless, you know."

Up until now, he's been looking all over the place, like he's been scanning the whole shop for weaknesses and vulnerabilities or something. But finally, he stops looking around and fixes me with a dark, impenetrable stare.

"There's been a crime wave here in Tanner Springs lately," he says simply. "Break-ins, burglaries. An arson, from the looks of it."

I vaguely remember reading something about that in the local paper a little bit ago. It didn't really seem like that big of a deal, though, even though the paper made it sound like the damn sky was falling. I mean, I'm from the city. Shit happens. Usually to people who aren't paying attention.

"Okay," I shrug. "So like I said, I'll be careful. Besides, what are they going to take? A few pounds of Kona and Blue Mountain to sell on the black market?" I joke.

"People have gotten hurt, Sydney," Gavin says quietly.

"I don't think a coffee shop is going to be high on the list of places to rob," I argue. "The most valuable thing in here is the espresso machine, and how would they even get it out of here without calling attention to themselves?"

"Yeah. *But* they could see a vulnerable woman, all alone in the shop, taking money out of the cash register," he says pointedly. "That's *almost* as easy as just breaking into a place without an alarm system and helping yourself to whatever you want."

"You know, Tanner Springs doesn't really seem like a hotbed of criminal activity. Some dumb kids robbing people for petty cash don't really scare me that much." I cock my head at him. "In fact, you and your club buddies seem like the most dangerous things around here. Shouldn't I be more afraid of having *you* in my shop while I'm all alone here?"

He pauses for a beat, his eyes still boring into mine.

"Yeah," he rumbles. One corner of his mouth turns up in a wicked half-smile that sends a sudden shiver up my spine. "You probably should."

12
SYDNEY

"What kind of cash do you usually have on hand in the register?"

We're standing behind the counter now, because for some reason, instead of kicking him out ten minutes ago like I should have, I'm still listening to him tell me how I'm putting myself in danger of being robbed or worse.

"Not a lot," I tell him. "You might not believe this, but a small-town coffee shop is not exactly a huge money-maker."

I don't know why I'm even answering his questions at this point. And I'm still pissed that he thinks he has a right to ask them, since they're none of his business.

"You have a safe?"

"Yes, I have a safe," I say, a touch angrily, my eyes flicking toward the back office.

"How much is usually in there?"

"Seriously," I complain. "These are exactly the kinds of questions you'd be asking if *you* were planning to rob me."

"If I were trying to rob you, I'd already have walked out the door with whatever I wanted."

"Is that right?" I stick out my chin.

"That's right." He takes a step closer. "You don't believe me?"

"I think you're underestimating my ability to defend myself."

Before I even know what's happening, Gavin's hands are locked around my upper arms, pulling me close enough to him that I'm basically immobilized.

"Really?" His voice turns low, slightly menacing. "Looks to me like you might be *overestimating* your ability."

A sharp spike of adrenaline jolts through me as my brain struggles to catch up to what just happened. He's definitely in control now, but I do my best to force my face not to show that I know it. Gavin's arms are like steel bands, and he's pinned me against the counter in such a way that I couldn't even move my legs enough to knee him in the groin if I had to.

"Well, sure," I say defiantly. There's a little wobble in my voice, and I hope he can't hear it. "You've got me *now*. But in a real-life situation, I never would have let you get this close to me in the first place."

"This *is* a real-life situation," he growls. "And you told me yourself, I seem like the most dangerous thing around here. But you still let me into your shop at night, and let the only other person here with you go home. We're locked in here now, just the two of us, and your phone and pepper spray — which you voluntarily told me all about — are out of your reach."

"I..." I fight to push down a tiny little spike of fear as I realize what he's saying. Gavin's eyes are boring into mine now, his face completely devoid of expression. I don't know how to respond. He's not *really*... I mean... *is* he? The possibility that I may have actually walked right into a trap like a complete idiot makes my heart begin to thud in my chest.

"Admit I'm right," he insists.

He's so close now that the rasp of his voice, deep and husky, sends an electric thrill through me. In spite of myself, my body is actually responding to him. To *this*. To his rough, callused hands. To the heat of his body, so close to mine. Everything feels like it's in hyper-focus right now. Down to his full, sensual lips that I can't help but realize are just inches from mine.

The little spike of adrenaline I felt just now wasn't fear. Not really. It was something else.

Desire. *Lust.*

"Admit it."

If he wants to do something to me, there's no way I can fight him off, I realize. *It's pointless to struggle. If he really is here to hurt me, then he's right. I walked right into it.*

And if he's here for something else, God help me but I probably won't resist at all.

"Okay," I whisper. "I admit it. You're right."

Gavin's hands release me, and suddenly he's three feet away from me, like none of this just happened. I lean weakly against the counter I was pinned against just moments ago. Taking a deep breath, I let it out raggedly but slowly, praying he won't notice just how much being that close to him has affected me.

"Now," he says, his voice suddenly all business again. "Let's talk about your safe. How much is usually in there?"

"Honestly," I say, as we stand in the back office. "If someone wanted all the money in the safe, I'd probably just give it to them. A few thousand dollars isn't worth enough for me to risk my life."

I've mostly recovered from Gavin's "lesson," but I'm still a little pissed off at myself. And at him. And a little flustered about my body's reaction to his. But I don't have the energy or the bravado to kick him out right now. It's like somehow, the last few minutes took all the fight out of me.

"Sure," he nods. "It's stupid to risk your life for something as unimportant as money. But that's not what I'm worried about. It's that we don't know the mental state of whoever is committing these break-ins." He turns to me. "You might think that just handing over the cash would be the end of it. But someone who's high, or even just nervous, might not be inclined to just let you go. And if they think you'll go to the cops, and be able to describe them, they might want to scare you enough so you'd think twice about that. Or worse."

I don't ask him to clarify what the *or worse* could be. A little tremor runs through me.

"Even with the front door locked, if you're back here when someone breaks in, you might not have enough time to call 911 or get your pepper spray out. And like I said, chemical agents don't always work." His jaw tenses. "And that's assuming they break in. They might just take an easier route, and wait until you come out — probably with the money from the till in your bag."

"So, basically, you're telling me that no matter what I do, I'm in danger of being robbed, or worse." I sigh and pull the hair tie out of my hair in frustration, raking my hands through my thick mane. "If that's the case, what's your point? Sounds like I can't avoid it, no matter what precautions I try to take."

"No. I'm not saying that. I mean, yes, there's always some risk. But it makes sense to try to mitigate that risk as much as possible."

"How?"

"Well, for one thing, don't take your money to the bank at night. Take it during the day, when there are more people around."

"Okay, but how does that stop me from getting hurt?" I say smugly. "I mean, am I supposed to carry a sign every night that says, 'The money from the till is in the safe'? The bad guys won't know I'm *not* carrying it."

"True," he admits.

"Ha!" I crow, pumping my fist.

"You like, that, huh? Proving me wrong?" For the first time, Gavin smiles. Not just a half-curve of the lip, or the hint of a smirk, but an actual *smile* that reveals even, white teeth and crinkles the corners of his eyes, totally transforming his whole face.

It's *dazzling*.

"Yeah. I like that," I smile back, ignoring the sudden thudding of my heart.

For a moment, we just stand there, not saying anything. It feels like something maybe passes between us. But then his eyes flick back toward the safe, and I tell myself it was just my imagination.

"So, you have a good point about the safe," he nods. "You should definitely start varying the times of day you go to the bank to make deposits. And don't do it at night anymore. But you need another kind of deterrent. I suggest a security camera or two. And especially a sign in the window that advertises you have them."

Even though I hate to admit it, all this talk about break-ins and danger has me just a tiny bit spooked, dammit. For a split second, I think about Devon. Would he ever try to take the money I left town with back from me? Would he actually track me down and try to make me give it back, even though he knows it was mine in the first place?

Would he really come to Tanner Springs to find me?

I try to ignore the little hairs that stand up on the back of my neck at the thought.

"You think so?" I ask, wavering.

"I do."

I take a deep breath, hold it, and let it out noisily. "Okay. You win. I'll look into it."

He smirks at me, eyes twinkling. "Good. I was going to win eventually, so I'm glad you decided to see reason."

"Oh, you were, were you?" I say sarcastically.

"You know I was." His tone turns teasing. "You're pretty goddamn stubborn, I'll give you that, but you've got nothing on me."

I snort. "God, isn't *that* the truth."

"It is," he agrees. "So, next time, let's just save ourselves the trouble, and you can just cut to the chase and agree with me. Deal?"

I can't help it. I laugh out loud. "That's… unlikely. But a guy can always dream, I guess."

This is so *weird*. It's so confusing, being around him. I can't read him at *all*. I have no idea how we went from him being sullen and demanding, to me being scared half out of my wits thinking he was about to rob me or worse, to now the two of us joking around like we actually like each other.

I mean, like we're *friends*, or something.

Still, this is way, *way* more comfortable than being scared of him — or being uncomfortably turned on by him — so I just go with it.

"I don't really know where to start, though," I continue. "I've never thought much about this stuff before. Do I just go to the security camera store and say, 'Hi, please hook me up with some sweet, sweet security'?"

"Tell you what," he suggests, leaning against my tiny desk. "Why don't you let me take care of it?"

"I couldn't," I begin, but he holds up a hand.

"Look, I'm going to win this argument eventually, remember? So you should just give up now and let it happen. You can reimburse me for the equipment. I'll install it for free."

As I open my mouth to argue, he seems to know what I'm about to say. He holds up his hand again, and gives me a look that says, *I've already won this argument, and you know it.*

I'm trying to think of some way to put him off — to convince him that I really will get around to contacting someone about coming to the shop and setting up cameras — when suddenly, my mind flashes back to Devon.

Dammit.

"Okay," I say.

13
BRICK

It never occurred to me to think of Sydney's coffee shop as one of the businesses that might be targeted. Not until I was riding past on the way home from the clubhouse tonight and saw that kid in there wiping down tables.

It's true that the Golden Cup might not be the most obvious target for whoever's doing these break-ins. But it's also true what I said: Anyone with criminal intent who walks or drives by this place at night is going to see Sydney in there and start thinking about ways to break in and overpower her.

Without some sort of protection, she's a sitting duck.

And a smoking hot one, at that.

Before I knew what I was doing, I was pounding my fist on the door, scaring the shit out of the girl and motioning for her to let me in.

The longer I'm alone with her in the locked shop, the less I'm worrying about someone robbing Sydney or vandalizing her store, and the more I'm picturing what a guy without a lot to lose might do when he sees a woman who looks like her — alone and just ripe for the taking.

Because even though Sydney seems like the kind of girl who can definitely handle herself in most situations, I don't think she really gets what kind of effect she has on the straight male population. How fucking crazy a girl like that can make a man who doesn't know how — or care — how to control himself. Sydney's curves could make a grown man sell his damn soul for a night with her. Those wicked, taunting eyes of hers — god *damn*. A man could lose himself forever in them. I want to see them flutter closed as she loses herself in pleasure. I want to bite her plump, ripe strawberry lips, to see if they taste as sweet as they look.

The thought of some fucking piece of shit *staring* at her through the plate glass, making *plans* of what he wants to do to her unwilling body… It makes me want to puke. And murder anyone who looks at Sydney the wrong way. I don't want to scare her needlessly. But I want her to be *careful*, for Christ's sake. And even though I believe she probably *is* for the most part, it's not enough. Not when I don't know who the hell is out there causing trouble in Tanner Springs, or why.

I didn't mean to frighten Sydney when I grabbed her in the back office. I wanted to show her how vulnerable she'd made herself by letting her guard down around me. Until I did it, it seemed like a good way to make the point. But as my hands closed around her upper arms and she realized she couldn't escape me if she tried, I realized I might have made a horrible mistake. For a second, as her wide, uncertain eyes looked up into mine, I felt like a fucking bastard — like some piece of shit mongrel of a human who gets off on scaring women for fun.

Worse — *much* worse — was the realization that she didn't know me well enough to be sure that I wasn't.

I opened my mouth to apologize, even though I was half-afraid she wouldn't believe me. But just as I did, I saw a flash of defiance transform her features. Her eyes seemed to bore straight through me, like she didn't buy my little game. Like she was calling my bluff, and didn't believe for a second I was about to hurt her.

The relief that flooded my veins came as a complete surprise, almost making me dizzy. I couldn't believe I'd done something so stupid. Something that came so close to making her never feel like she could trust me.

And all because I wanted to protect her, ironically.

I let go of her and took a step back, even more pissed off at myself because I was hard as fucking iron from being so close to her, even for a few seconds. The thing is, I could have almost sworn by the look on her face, by the blush on the skin of her neck — by the way her breathing sped up a little bit when she locked eyes with me — that Sydney was as turned on as I was. But I wasn't about to take the risk of being wrong. And even if I wasn't, trying something at that moment was about the worst fucking idea in the history of bad timing.

So, I forced myself to think about anything — absolutely *anything* — but fucking Sydney in the back room of her coffee shop. I promised myself I wouldn't ever make a fucked-up mistake like that again. And that I would make goddamn sure she was as safe as humanly possible, to make up for the shitty thing I'd done. In my own mind, at least.

I don't know what finally makes Sydney stop arguing with me about her needing more security at the shop, but I'm not about to waste any time when she does.

"I'll come back tomorrow night to set up a camera and show you how to work it," I tell her. "You'll be here?"

"Yes. Just me." She looks at me and narrows her eyes, like she's expecting me to bitch about her being alone in the shop at night again, but I decide not to push it for now. She's agreed to let me help her. That's the most important part for now.

"Okay. Same time, roughly?" I glance around the room for a clock, but I don't see one.

"We close at eight," she tells me.

"I'll be here at five to."

94

She moves to let me out, but I'm not leaving until she leaves with me. With a huff of indignation, Sydney finishes up the last of her closing chores as I wait. She puts the cash drawer in the safe, and the two of us go out the back, her locking the door behind us.

"See you tomorrow," I say when we get to her car. It's the only one parked in the tiny darkened back lot.

"M-hm," she grumbles, and slides into the driver's side. I wait until she's started the engine — noting with satisfaction that she automatically locks the car from the inside when she gets in — and drives off into the night.

I walk around the block to the front to my bike, my head full of Sydney, my nostrils full of the scent of her shampoo. My cock is still at half-staff in my pants, and I'm too keyed up to head home to the lake house. So, instead, I head toward the clubhouse. I'll work off some steam and spend the night in my apartment there.

Half an hour later, I've stripped down to a loose, faded T-shirt and I'm in the club's weight room. Everyone else is out in the bar drinking, playing pool, and raising hell, so I've got the place to myself. The steady boom of bass guitar drifts toward me from the sound system in the main room. I'm benching as much weight as I can tolerate, veins bulging out of my neck as I grit my teeth and swear to myself.

After a little while, someone comes in, as the music swells louder through the open doorway.

"Hey, brother," Angel's voice says. "You're missing the party."

I grunt loudly, giving the barbell a final push and setting it above me on the rack. "Yeah," I mutter, and sit up. "Needed a little stress relief. The non-alcoholic kind."

Angel takes a seat on the bench beside me. "Hey, I wanted to give you a heads up. Apparently, Rock is gonna go talk to Oz tomorrow. To see if the Death Devils have been dealing with similar shit as we have."

"Alone?" It's not exactly unheard of for Rock to go to a meet without at least some of his officers, but it is pretty unusual.

"Yeah." Angel is silent for a moment. "I asked him who he was taking, but he cut me off. Told me to leave it alone."

Whoa. That *is* unusual. When a president is gone, the VP is in absolute charge of the club. For Rock to not be forthcoming with his own vice-president… well, it's pretty damn troubling. Even if nothing's going on.

We sit like that, without talking, for maybe a minute. There's a feeling of foreboding between us, but it's not something that's very easy to talk about. Loyalty to and respect for the club president is fundamental to our code as brothers and officers of the Lords of Carnage. It's one thing to challenge an idea the president has during church, or to offer an opinion on a decision that has to be made. But it's another thing to be questioning Rock's actions behind his back.

And even more than that: I get the feeling that we've both been privately questioning more than just one or two of Rock's actions. Even though Angel hasn't said a word to me, the look on is face tells me he's been thinking some of the same things I have.

Angel is starting to question his *judgment*.

For Angel to say anything to me about this — even if he hasn't actually *said* anything — is a testament to how concerned he is. Because although Rock seems to have his own doubts about whether Angel's got his back lately, the truth is that Angel is as good a VP as Rock could ever ask for. I admit, I've questioned Angel in the past. Back when his dad was still the mayor, I wasn't always sure Angel's loyalty to the club would stand up to his sense of duty to his family. But I'm man enough to admit I was wrong about that. Angel's as solid as they come, and his determination to do the right thing by all of us is something I never should have questioned.

The silence is still hanging in the air between us. Once one of us says anything, we've started a real conversation about Rock that goes beyond what we've said to ourselves in our heads. And we both know it.

"I don't like this," I tell him finally.

He nods once and stands. "Neither do I."

Then he's gone.

I pump iron for a few more minutes, but now my thoughts are swirling with all the things Angel and I *didn't* say to each other just now. With an angry grunt, I finally throw down the dumbbell I've been using for curls and stand up from the bench. This isn't working.

Pushing open the door to the weight room, I step out into the hall and walk through the bar, past the brothers who raise their bottles at me and offer me a drink, and the club girls who tilt their heads coyly at me in silent invitation. I ignore them all and head upstairs to my apartment, where I pour myself a couple shots of whiskey and down them one after the other. Then I turn off the lights, strip down, and climb into bed. I close my eyes and give in to the thoughts of Sydney that have been with me all night. Within seconds, I'm hard, and I wrap my hand around my throbbing cock and stroke myself to a shuddering release. It's not nearly enough, but at least it helps me fall into a restless, troubled sleep.

14
SYDNEY

Gavin insists on installing two cameras at the shop, even though I tell him it's overkill. There's one trained on the entrance, so anyone who approaches the place will be recorded, whether they come in or not. Then he puts a second one above the entrance on the inside, angled so it records everything that happens in the main room of the shop and the hallway.

We're standing in the back alley now, where my car is parked, and he's muttering to himself.

"I should have brought a motion sensor light for back here," he's muttering to himself. "And another camera. I'll come back tomorrow and get that set up for you."

"Gavin," I sigh, "Don't you think this is all a bit much? I mean, for God's sake. You're acting like this place is Fort Knox or something."

"Can't be too careful," he replies as he stands at the edge of the tiny parking area, clearly calculating where to install the light.

"I don't know about *that*," I snark to myself and shake my head. But it's no use arguing. Gavin told me last night he was stubborn, and holy crap, he wasn't kidding. Part of me is sorry I ever agreed to let him do any of this in the first place. Still, I can't help but admit to myself that I *do* feel just a little bit safer.

When everything is set up and he's tested the cameras to make sure they're working, he pulls out a couple of signs for the front and back doors that warn any potential criminals the shop is under twenty-four hour video surveillance. "The signs actually do the lion's share of the work as a deterrent," he tells me. "So having them someplace prominent is important."

"Yeah. So prominent that my customers are going to see them and wonder why I'm so freaking paranoid," I joke.

He ignores me, of course. While he's placing the signs, I wander over behind the counter and mentally go over my closing checklist to make sure I haven't forgotten anything. Then I absently pick up a small stack of recipes I've printed out and start leafing through them.

"What'cha looking at?" he says, startling me enough that I jump and let out a little squeak. He's somehow come up behind me without making a sound.

"Dammit, don't scare me like that!" I wheeze, putting a hand to my chest. "I'm looking at kolache recipes."

"Really?" Gavin's mouth turns up at the corners. "What for?"

"That damn grumpy guy came in again with his friends this morning," I fume. "It's the third time he's been here, and he's still acting like he's practically being forced to come here at gunpoint." I jut out my chin. "But I've decided I'm going to wear him down if it kills me. I'm going to make him some kolaches and surprise him."

Gavin smirks. "You know he's just gonna tell you they aren't any good."

"I don't care," I declare. "If he does, then I'll know he's just an ungrateful jerk, and I won't care any more what he thinks. But at least I'll know I tried."

"You're a determined one," he says mildly. "Good luck with that."

"Thanks." I select the recipe that looks the most promising and move it to the top of the pile.

"So," he continues, glancing around. "I'm all done here. You?"

"Yeah. I've got a couple more things I could do, but I think I'll leave them for tomorrow morning." I take a deep breath and give him a smile. "So, thanks for doing this. I mean, quite honestly, you were a complete pain in the ass about it, but now that it's done…" I shrug. "I guess it can't hurt anything to take a little extra precaution."

"Jesus, finally," he chuckles, the sound deep and sexy in his throat. "I thought you'd never admit it."

"Don't make me regret it," I warn him.

His chuckle turns into a deep-throated laugh. It reminds me of the first time I ever actually saw him actually *smile*, and my stomach does this little flip-flop thing that makes me feel a little sick and a little giddy at the same time.

"So. Look," he says when he's done laughing. "If you're done here, and I'm done here, come get a drink with me at the Lion's Tap."

The flip-flop thing my stomach's doing turns into a full-on cannonball off the high dive.

"Um, I don't know…" I say vaguely.

Yes, I fully admit — if only to myself — that I find Gavin insanely hot. To the point where it's a near-constant struggle to maintain my composure around him . But the idea of sitting with him in a crowded bar, on an almost-date even if it isn't really one, seems like an even stupider idea than being completely one-hundred percent alone with him in a locked coffee shop. Add in a little liquid courage, and this is definitely *not* a path I should not be going down.

"One drink," he says, and winks at me. "It's the least you can do to thank me, you know."

"You mean you're gonna let me pay?" I say in astonishment.

"Hell no!" he laughs. "Come on. You know I'm not gonna take no for an answer."

In the end, I give in, but only on the condition that one's my limit. A few minutes later, we're sitting at the bar at the Lion's Tap, a beer in front of him and a gin and tonic for me. I've never been here before, though I've walked by a number of times. It's kind of dark, and there are a few rowdy groups over on the other side of the room playing darts and yelling at each other. But over here it's quieter, almost intimate.

"So. You said you're from New Jersey. What brought you to Tanner Springs?" Gavin asks me.

I'm impressed he remembers that detail, but I'm not particularly interested in telling him my life story. "Oh, I heard about the town from a relative," I say, waving a vague hand. "My great-aunt. She didn't live here, but she knew someone who did and came here to visit sometimes. She said it was a really nice place. So, when I was looking to get out of Atlantic City and go someplace a little quieter, this seemed as good a place as any to start."

"Atlantic City, huh? You grow up there?"

"Sort of," I murmur softly.

"What's that?" he cocks his head at me.

"Sort of," I say louder. "My dad was… in the resort and casino business." *Ha. That's putting it kindly.*

"That so?" He frowns. "Must have been kind of a weird place to live as a kid."

You don't know the half of it. "Yeah. It's a weird place all around. One day I decided I had enough of The Big Hustle. A new beginning, you know? A new life." I lift a shoulder.

Gavin gives me a strange look. "Yeah. I know what you mean."

"That's right," I remember. "You said you came here after the military. Marines, right?"

"Yeah." He leans back. "By the time I got out, there wasn't much for me back home. So I decided to take my buddy Gunner up on his offer to come down here. Get to know the club. See if I was interested in patching in."

"'Patching in'?" I ask, wrinkling my brow.

"Joining up. Becoming a member."

I consider this. "What's it like, being in a motorcycle club?"

"It's a full-time job," he replies. "More than that. It's a brotherhood. A family."

I chew over his words. "What do you do, other than that?" I ask. "Like, for work?"

"The club owns a custom bike and auto design shop. I work there with a bunch of the other brothers. And, a few other things here and there."

"'A few other things,'" I repeat with a smirk. "Like, a few other not quite legal things?"

"Not so much at the moment." He winks at me.

"So, basically, the club's your life." I'm half-joking, but he doesn't smile.

"It is," he agrees. "Getting patched into a club, you take an oath of loyalty. It's a lifelong commitment, in most cases. A choice you don't take on lightly."

It's funny, hearing him talk about life in the club. He probably wouldn't believe it, but I'm a lot more familiar with that kind of existence than he thinks.

It sounds a little bit like the life I left behind in Atlantic City, in a way. It's worlds apart from what most people think of as normal. In a way, it was sort of a secret society. A closed community, where even if you didn't personally know another 'member,' you almost certainly knew *of* them.

Except in the world I left behind, there was no such thing as loyalty to *anybody* but yourself.

"Hey," he murmurs, jolting me out of my thoughts. "You went somewhere else for a second."

"Sorry." I look down, feeling my cheeks flush. "Just remembering something."

"Your drink's empty," he points out. "Want another one?"

I shake my head, though I'm tempted to say yes. I kind of like talking to him like this, actually. On neutral territory, he's less… intimidating. Almost charming, actually.

"No, I better get going. I have to be to the shop tomorrow morning by six."

"Gotcha." He tosses a bill on the counter and stands up. "I'll walk you to your car." I start to protest, but he stops me. "I'm walking you to your car, and that's final."

We leave the bar and walk outside into the slightly humid night air. The moon is hanging low and red in the sky, just over the rooftops beyond downtown. The two of us walk in near silence toward my car, which is still parked in back of the Golden Cup.

"You know, Gavin, you can't just follow me around constantly, protecting me," I finally joke, because the relative quiet feels too weird after the noisiness of the bar.

"So about that," he rumbles. "What's with calling me Gavin? I told you, my name's Brick."

"No, you told me your *club nickname* is Brick," I correct him. "I'm not in your club. Besides, I like the name Gavin. It suits you."

He grunts, but doesn't say anything more.

"Have you gotten that fire extinguisher fixed yet?" he eventually growls.

"I haven't had time." I don't want to admit the thought hadn't occurred to me. It would just give him more fuel for the fire. *Ha — fuel for the fire!* I snort to myself at my own private joke.

"What are you laughing about?" Gavin cocks a brow at me.

"Nothing."

"Nothing? You're not going to let me in on the joke?"

We're at the parking lot now. When we get to my car, Brick leans against my driver's side door, to stop me from opening it.

"It's not important. Just a dumb thing that occurred to me." He still doesn't move. "Are you going to let me get into my car?"

"Are you going to look around and check the area to make sure no one's hiding in the shadows, waiting for you?" His eyes are reproachful.

"Of course I would have, if *you* weren't here," I huff.

"Sure. That's what you *say*."

I can't tell if he's teasing me, or if he doesn't believe me. And suddenly, it almost doesn't matter, because I'm *furious*. And weirdly *sad*, or something. We were just having this kind of nice, almost *normal* time back there, and now he's back to being Mister Judgmental. I don't know why I care, but I actually sort of *liked* talking to him back in the bar, and on the way back here. It felt… nice. And now, I just feel like a stupid child he's reprimanding again. It's so *demeaning*. Like I'm not someone anyone could take seriously.

Fuck it, I think. I'm not going to put up with this bullshit anymore.

"Gavin, god *damn* it, I'm seriously fucking *sick* of you treating me like an idiot child!" I half-shout. Anyone in earshot could hear us right now, but I just don't care. "Literally ever since the first actual conversation we had, you've been telling me how stupid and thoughtless and inattentive I am — coming into *my* business and telling me what to do with it. I'm twenty-five years old and I'm still standing, so I must have figured out a few things on my own. I may not do things exactly the way you want me to, but it's not your choice how I do *anything*."

"Is that so?" he teases me.

I don't know how I was expecting him to react, but his amused grin almost sends me into orbit.

I want to fly at him — pound my fists against his chest, rage at him with all my might — but goddamnit, that's just going to make him patronize me even *more*. Suddenly, I want nothing more than for him to just be gone. Anywhere, just away from me. The blood boiling in my veins turns to ice.

"Please, step away from my car," I tell him rigidly, my jaw clenched to stop me from screaming. "I'm going home. And I'm finished with this conversation."

The twinkle in his eye fades, as he seems to finally understand I'm serious, and *seriously* angry.

"Sydney." His voice drops, low and husky. "I know you can take care of yourself. I'm not doing this because I think you're a child."

His tone is so soft, so suddenly intimate, that it almost feels like a caress on my skin. I shiver a little, and try to shake it off.

"Oh, yeah?" I retort, but it comes out a little trembly. "Then why—?"

He takes half a step forward. I freeze in my spot as he raises a hand to graze my cheek with his thumb.

"Because I think there's something serious going on in Tanner Springs. And I don't know what the fuck it is yet. I'm trying to protect you because I'm worried about you." His hand moves behind my neck and fists in my hair, tugging just slightly until my head is tilted up to his. "And because I've been wanting to do this since the first day I saw you."

15
SYDNEY

The moment just before he kisses me — when his face is just *inches* away from mine — feels like it goes on forever.

His dark eyes are locked on mine. They look hungry, almost *savage*. So much so that I feel like my skin is melting from the heat that's arcing between us.

I feel his fist tighten in my hair. Then, just as my eyes start to flutter closed, his mouth comes down on mine. The kiss starts out hard, demanding, but almost immediately Gavin pulls back — so slightly it's almost imperceptible, but it changes the rhythm completely. He kisses me slowly, searchingly. His tongue grazes my bottom lip, like soft fire, and with a sharp gasp I open my mouth to his, the wanting making me suddenly dizzy with the force of it.

He pushes me back against the car, his body pressing into mine. I realize I'm hardly managing to breathe. Every nerve ending in my body is aflame at his touch, alive and yielding to the hard muscularity of him. A sharp throb begins between my legs as his tongue curls around mine, teasing, toying, insisting. My hands reach up on their own and cling to the fabric of his shirt, pulling him toward me, never wanting this to end.

Gavin grunts low in his throat and tugs my head back, exposing the flesh of my neck. He begins to nip and lick at the skin, sending electric jolts down my body straight to my core. I moan, loudly, and roll my hips toward him, my body instinctively seeking what it knows is there. I almost gasp when I find it — the hard, delicious length of his erection, which I suddenly *need* him to press into me. I need him to relieve just a little of the ache — an ache that's only getting stronger and more insistent with every second he touches me.

As if he knows exactly what my body is asking, Brick's other arm goes around me, lifting me up and pressing his hips into mine. I barely manage not to cry out at how good it feels when the friction of his hardness grazes me *exactly* where I need it. I can feel myself soaking through my panties, and that thought leads to the thought of him pressing the huge length of his cock inside me, filling me, and...

"I'll see you tomorrow," Gavin growls into my neck, releasing me.

I blink and open my eyes, trying to control the sound of my panting and my heaving breasts.

"What?" I stammer.

"I'll see you tomorrow. To put in the motion sensor light and the last camera." He glances down at my car. "Get in. I'll stay here until you're on your way."

In a daze, I do what he says, unlocking my car with a shaky hand. I'm not about to *beg* him to keep kissing me, after all — I have more pride than that — and I'm too confused to ask him why he stopped. I'm pretty sure it wasn't because the kiss was bad or because I smell or anything, because he's still looking at me with those hungry, feral eyes as I slide into the driver's seat and tremblingly pull the door closed.

Gavin nods once as he hears me press the door lock button and watches me put on my seatbelt. A tiny, tiny vestige of my anger at his overprotectiveness threads through my veins, but I'm far too gone for it to reach me. I feel dizzy from his kiss, like I could melt into a quaking puddle right here in the seat.

I watch myself turn the key in the ignition and put the car into drive, almost like I'm seeing someone else do it. On the way home, my skin feels like it's *buzzing*, almost as though someone's running an electrical current through me. The feeling lasts as I park my car and let myself into the tiny house I'm renting. Inside, I look around in a daze, almost as though I've walked into someone else's life by mistake. Everything feels different, like it's in hyper-focus.

It's weird as hell.

When I finally start to snap out of it a bit, I can't help but laugh at myself a little. God, I'm acting like a teenager who's never even been kissed before. It's not like I haven't had my share of sexual partners — though, let's be honest, I have *never* had a kiss that affected me quite like that. My body is still *thrumming* with excitement, the memory of his lips still on mine. I can still feel the tension of his body — the raw power I could sense in the hardness of his muscles — but what took me completely by surprise was the unexpected tenderness of his kiss. Even though somehow *right* behind the gentle pressure of his lips was something that was just waiting to be unleashed. Gavin held himself back. Why, I'm not sure. But I don't think it was because he didn't want more.

I get ready for bed mechanically, barely registering it as I pull off my clothes and toss them in the hamper. I already know what I'm going to do when I slide between the sheets. As soon as the light's off and I'm in bed, I reach into the tiny drawer of my bedside table and pull out my vibrator, my breath speeding up slightly. I haven't had sex since before I moved to Tanner Springs. I've definitely made use of battery-operated help since then. But I haven't been nearly as turned on — as desperate for release — as I am right now, since…

Well, honestly, I'm not sure I've *ever* been this turned on.

I move my legs apart, and imagine that the vibrations sliding along my slick folds are his fingers caressing me. Then his tongue, teasing me expertly as I arch my back off the mattress and moan softly. I reach up and pinch one nipple, pulling in a sharp breath as I realize how close I already am. I want to draw it out as long as possible but I can't, I need it too much, and as I shudder through my orgasm I surprise myself by crying out Gavin's name in the dark. I fall asleep to the memory of his lips on mine.

*   *   *

Instead of dreaming about Gavin, though, it's Devon who comes to haunt me in the night.

It's a gambling dream. I haven't had one of those in months. In it, I'm playing roulette — not blackjack, which was my game back in the day. For some reason, my dad's the croupier. He looks like he did when he was younger, not prematurely aged by the cancer like he was at the end.There are other people at the table, but I only recognize Devon. He's wearing his standard black shirt and black jeans. His sharp, angular face is tense with concentration, hungry to win — a look I know only too well.

I hate roulette. I don't know why I'm at this table. It's a game where you almost always lose to the table, eventually. The house edge is high — sometimes over five percent. That's higher than blackjack, craps, or baccarat. So I know I'm going to have to be careful if I want to walk away from the table with my money.

I'm not sure why it doesn't occur to me to just take my chips and go to the blackjack table. Or hell, just leave the casino. Because that's what I want to do. But in the dream I somehow *know* that they won't let me out of here unless I play, at least once. I tell myself that if I just place one bet, that will be it, and I can go.

Roulette gives you the chance to win thirty-five times your bet. In this way, roulette is more like slots -- one single bet can win a lot. It's also like slots in that the house edge is very high.

I place an even money bet, on numbers one through eighteen. Atlantic City has a special rule that reduces the house edge to 2.7% on even money bets, so it's my best strategy to play conservative and move on.

Devon makes a Street Bet — a set of three numbers, which will pay out eleven to one if he wins. All of the numbers he chooses are between one and eighteen. Which means if he wins, I win. If he loses, so do I.

He has almost three times as many chips as I do, and he puts them all in, divided up evenly among the three numbers. I bet the table minimum and no more. Since it's an even money payoff. I won't make much off of it even if I win, but I don't care. All I want is to get out of here.

An almost claustrophobic crush tightens my chest as I watch my father release the ball. I hate having Devon's fate linked to mine, even momentarily. A nervous churning starts deep in my gut as we all watch the ball fly around the wheel, ricocheting off the numbers with a ratcheting sound.

The ball lands on twenty-four, black. We both lose. I realize I've been holding my breath, and let it out as silently as I can. I'm almost relieved by losing, because if I'd won, I know I'd be tempted to bet again. I scoop all the chips I have left into my bag and turn from the table — away from both Devon and my father — without a word. I walk as fast as I can without running, but suddenly cry out in pain as Devon grabs my hair and pulls me back.

"Don't walk away with my money, bitch," he rasps against my ear. His breath is thick with smoke and booze.

I scream loudly, hoping someone will see what's happening and help me. But as I look around wildly, I know it's no use. Even though almost every casino I've even been in is always packed with people, in my dream there's no one in sight, and the room's as black and deep as a tunnel. I launch my purse backward, throwing it as far behind me as I can, and then wrench my hair away from Devon and run as fast as I can, hoping I'm running toward the entrance, and light, and freedom…

With a start, I wake up in my darkened bedroom. Not a hint of morning light is coming through the window, and the silence of a world asleep is almost deafening. I sit upright and listen to my own jagged breathing, and try to shake off the demons of my sleep.

You're here, I repeat in my head like a mantra with every breath. *You're here.*

After way too many minutes, I fall back onto the bed, but I can tell sleep isn't going to find me again tonight. So instead, I roll over and stand up, resigned.

A long, hot shower's the best thing I can imagine to clear my head. And then off to the shop, to lose myself in mixing, baking, and brewing. To be Sydney Banner, of Tanner Springs — and leave Syd Banner of Atlantic City firmly back in the past, where she belongs.

16
BRICK

Pulling away from Sydney — resisting the urge to take her up against her car in the darkened parking lot — was just about the hardest fucking thing I've ever done.

I didn't even know I was going to pull away until I'd already done it. I could tell she was confused as hell when I stepped back and told her good night. Hell, my cock was confused, too. Sydney was ready for me — fuck, the way she was moaning and grinding herself against me told me she was *desperate* for it. I stopped something we *both* wanted to happen. And I wanted it so bad it was practically driving me crazy, imagining what she would taste like when I spread her tight little thighs apart and plunged my tongue into that sweet pussy of hers.

Even as I ride back to my place with a raging damn hard-on — my cock yelling at me for letting the moment go — in my gut, I know it was the right decision.

I'm still pissed at myself for scaring her in the coffee shop that night. I'm used to being in control in the bedroom — hell, I *demand* it — but I'm not taking what I want from someone who doesn't want it, too. Last night in the alley, she was vulnerable. And even though I knew she wanted it as much as I did, I sure as hell didn't want her associating fucking me with getting attacked in the dark by some piece of shit.

I'm going to have Sydney. I know that as surely as I know anything. But I'm gonna make damn sure that it's on her turf, and that she knows exactly what she's agreeing to. I'm going to make her ask.

Hell, I'm gonna make her *beg*.

The next morning, I wait until Sydney's morning rush is over to show up to the shop. There are only two customers in the Golden Cup when I arrive, both of them sitting alone at tables by the window. I push open the door, the now-familiar bell announcing my arrival. Sydney looks up from filling a small container of something, and colors when she sees it's me.

She looks a little tired this morning, the flush of her cheeks standing out against the pale of her skin. She's not wearing makeup, I don't think, and it just makes her more gorgeous, more *her*. Like she's just a little closer to naked without anything on her face.

"Morning," I nod to her, stepping up to the counter. I hold up the bag I'm carrying. "I've got that camera and motion sensor light for the back."

She looks a little flustered, and I know she's thinking about last night. It's fucking adorable.

"I thought you were coming back tomorrow night!" she murmurs.

"I said I'd see you tomorrow. This is tomorrow."

Her eyes flick toward the customers. "Okay," she says, giving a slight nod. "You can go back and do whatever you need to do. The back door locks from the inside, so leave it open so you can get back in."

I barely hear what she says. I'm too focused on the pale pink of her lips, and the memory of how they tasted last night. Instantly I'm hard, and I shift the bag subtly in front of my crotch.

"I'll have it done in less than an hour," I tell her, and walk down the hall toward the back. I left my drill and other tools in her office, and I go in and grab them, looking at the small desk and chuckling as I get an idea for later.

I'm done with the installations in forty-five minutes. This morning before I came here, I set the camera up to transmit to my phone, like I did with the others. If anything happens, I'll be able to access the video wherever I am, whenever I need to.

I only feel a small twinge of guilt that I'm not telling Sydney this.

When I get back inside, one of her customers has left. The other, a thin, pinched-looking middle-aged man, is tapping softly on a laptop, ear buds in his ears and an empty cup on the table in front of him.

Sydney turns toward me expectantly, looking a little less rattled than she was earlier.

"I'll take my payment in coffee," I tell her. "The usual."

She gives me a small, shy smile. "Okay. But I'm out of blueberry muffins this morning. You want to test something out for me?"

"What's that?"

One corner of her mouth quirks up, revealing a small dimple I never noticed before. "A kolache."

It's good. The dough is golden and puffy, and in the middle of the round pastry is a little mound of what turns out to be a kind of sweet cream cheese. It's fucking good with the coffee.

"If that old bastard doesn't like this, there's no saving him," I tell her when I've swallowed the first bite.

Sydney beams. "I made some with poppy seed topping, too. They're in the oven now."

"Sounds delicious." I mean it. I've had enough of Sydney's pastries by know to know she's really good at this.

"Maybe if you play your cards right, I'll let you taste one of those, too," she replies saucily. I don't know why, but there's something about the look on her face she gets when she decides to tease me. It makes me want to carry her into the back room and do every filthy thing I can think of to her.

"How'd you learn how to bake?" I ask her instead. I almost expect her face to cloud over, like it usually does when I ask her a personal question. But instead, she actually gives me something like an answer.

"My mom wasn't really around when I was a kid," she tells me. "My dad raised me. I'm an only child, so I spent a lot of time alone, at home when he was at... work. Pretty often I lived in neighborhoods that didn't have a lot for a kid to do. So," she shrugs, "What does a bored and hungry kid with a sweet tooth do? Learn to bake stuff."

"That, or learn to shoplift," I smirk, "Like I did."

In the kitchen, the oven timer goes off.

"Should I be leaving you unsupervised in here?" she smirks.

"Remember, we're under video surveillance," I murmur, looking up toward the camera trained on us. "I could never get away with it."

Sydney heads back to check on her kolaches. I finish mine in silence, thinking about her ass. A minute or so later, the skinny guy closes his laptop and packs it up into a shoulder bag. He leaves his empty cup on his table and leaves. As the bell rings behind him, I stand and go back into the kitchen.

"Your last customer is gone," I murmur against Sydney's ear as I come up behind her.

My lips graze the sensitive skin of her neck. I hear her pull in a shallow breath.

I wrap one arm around her and pull her back against me, letting her feel how hard I already am. Sliding a hand into her jeans, under her panties, I dip a finger into her wetness. She's fucking soaked. She gasps.

"Close the shop," I growl.

"What?" she says breathlessly.

"Close the shop. Now."

It's an order, but this is Sydney's place. She's under no obligation to follow it, and she knows it.

She turns her head back toward me, her lips parted. I feel her hips arch back, pressing her ass against my cock.

"Okay," she whispers.

I watch her as she moves to the front door, turns the sign to 'closed,' and flips the lock.

When she comes back, I meet her at the entrance to the hallway.

"Office," I command.

She doesn't even hesitate. She bites her bottom lip, eyes wide and dark, and then continues on back, knowing I'm following right behind her. When she reaches the office, she turns around to face me. She reaches behind her to the desk, steadying herself. Her lips are parted, breathing shallow. She's fucking ready for me. She *wants* this. I know she does. But I need to hear her say it.

"Did you touch yourself last night and think about me?" I growl, my cock so hard I'm half afraid it's going to split the zipper on my jeans.

"Yes," she whispers.

"You want this."

"Yes," she whispers again.

"Say it."

"I want this."

"Take off your clothes," I order. "I want to watch you."

She's wearing one of those simple, tiny T-shirts that show off her tits. I watch, my cock aching, as she pulls it over her head, revealing a lacy pink bra underneath. My cock throbs harder as she reaches back and unhooks the bra, then slides it down her arms to reveal gorgeous, round globes with taut pink buds the same color as her lips. *Fuck*. It's killing me not to reach out and take her tits in my hands, but I'm enjoying the agony.

Sydney's skin is flushed and gorgeous. I don't take my eyes off her for a second.

"Lose the jeans," I tell her as I pull off my own shirt.

She does as I tell her, her eyes locked on my chest and arms. I realize she's looking at my tattoos, her gaze moving from one to the other as she kicks off her shoes, then wriggles out of her jeans and steps out of them.

She's standing in front of me now, naked except for a pair of thin panties.

"Fuck," I growl. "You're goddamn gorgeous, Sydney."

I've waited as long as I can. Unzipping my jeans, I push them down and my cock springs free, painfully hard. For just a moment, I take myself in my hand and stroke, slowly, while I look at her, and try not to groan out loud. Jesus fuck, this feels good. I'm torn between just bending her over the desk and fucking her senseless, and taking my time with her. But the one thing I can't risk is having someone knock on the door outside and her grabbing her clothes and running out to open the shop before I've finished with her. I make my decision.

"Sit on the desk," I order her. She immediately does what she's told. I move between her legs, the head of my cock brushing again her wetness. Sydney throws her head back and groans, her legs spreading. I lean down and kiss her, my tongue probing deeply in her mouth as I tease her already swollen lower lips. She whimpers and strains toward me.

"This is just the beginning, sweetheart," I rasp, my lips moving lower, to the sensitive skin of her neck. Her pulse is beating like the wings of a bird. "This is just the beginning of everything I'm going to do to you."

I reach up with one hand and cup her full breast, my thumb going to her sensitive nipple. I brush against her skin with the rough pad, and she gasps and arches her chest toward me. "Gavin," she moans, her tone urgent. "Oh, God…"

Something flips low in my belly when she says my name. That throaty voice, so full of need, saying a name that almost no one knows. The name that only she uses. It pulls at something deep, like she's reaching inside, to a place no one else knows to look for.

Whatever it is, it's tied straight to my dick.

It would be so fucking easy to slide my aching cock inside of her, to bury myself up to the hilt. She's so ready for me. But I've been waiting for too long to taste her, and I can't wait anymore. I press her back until she's lying on the desk, and push her up until her feet are resting on top. I spread her knees and bend down to lick and nip at the sensitive skin of her thighs. I can feel the exact moment that she realizes what I'm about to do: her muscles tense in anticipation, her hips angling up to meet my mouth.

I growl low in my throat and swipe my tongue slowly the length of her pussy. *Good God, she tastes sweet.* She shudders and cries out, her thighs falling open even more. I swipe again, then plunge my tongue deep inside her, tasting her, learning her, listening to her body as she whimpers and thrusts toward me. I want to take my time, but more than anything, I want to hear her come, want to *feel* her come on my tongue. I lick and tease, and Sydney's hands clutch desperately at the desk. Her head rolls from side to side, her cries getting louder and higher. Suddenly, with a gasp and a shout, she convulses, her entire body shaking as her orgasm takes her.

I continue to lap at her until she begins to quiet. Then I bend down and grab my jeans, pulling a condom out of my wallet and sliding it over my shaft. Just that amount of contact makes me stifle a groan, I'm that hard, and then I'm sliding my cock against her soaking entrance and she's begging me to push inside her, to fill her. I sink inside her hot channel as slowly as I can stand it, but then Sydney's moaning and thrashing again and I grab her hips and start to thrust, hard, harder, and I feel her pussy tightening around me as she comes a second time, and I shout her name and empty myself inside her, coming so hard I think for a second I might pass out.

17
BRICK

"Oh, my God," Sydney's panting as I pull her up, still inside her, and wrap my arms around her. I kiss her deeply, and she giggles. "You taste like me," she murmurs.

"Fucking delicious, isn't it?" I say.

"That was…" she takes a deep, shuddering breath. "Wow."

"Wow is fucking right," I agree. "About time we got around to that."

"I'll never look at this office the same way again," she smirks, shaking her head as she looks down at the desk.

"Good." I kiss her. "You'll be wet and ready for me every time you balance your cash register from now on."

Sydney's skin flushes. "I should open the shop back up," she murmurs. "I've never closed during the day before."

I bend down and grab her clothes, then hand them to her. We get dressed in silence, but it's not particularly awkward. Her ponytail has come mostly undone, and she pulls out the hair tie and rakes her fingers through her tresses, putting it up again. "How do I look?" she asks.

"Like sex on a plate. Minus the plate."

"The idea is to *not* look like sex," she informs me, smoothing her hair.

"Well, I think that's a losing battle," I tell her. "But suit yourself. You look fine. No one will ever know you were back here getting your brains fucked out just moments ago."

That earns me a snort. "Romantic."

"Hey, fucking *is* romantic," I protest. "It's just that instead of bringing you flowers, I brought you a surveillance cam."

I let her go out and open up first, so she won't be embarrassed if anyone's waiting outside. A couple minutes later, I follow her. I walk out into the main shop just as someone else is coming through the door.

"I'll see you later," I murmur into her hair. "I gotta go take care of some stuff."

"Okay," she murmurs back. I turn to go, then look back at her one last time. She gives me a radiant smile — so radiant I realize I don't think I've ever actually *seen* her smile like that before. It's like a goddamn present, knowing I'm the one who put it there.

I ride over to the clubhouse in time for church, feeling like I just slew a fucking dragon.

* * *

"None of the business owners I talked to had any information for us that we don't already know," Striker is saying. "None of them had working video surveillance, either, but a couple of them said they were planning to install it because of the break-in. All of them seemed a little suspicious of me coming to talk to them at first, but in the end I think I was able to convince them that the Lords weren't involved, and that we're serious about wanting to help keep this shit away from Tanner Springs."

"That's about what I got, too," Hawk says. "It was a smart move, us going to them directly. Good public relations. Glen, the guy who owns Ace Liquor, told me to thank the club for reaching out."

It's nice to have a little good news. Two more places have been robbed or vandalized in the last week. One looks like it probably wasn't connected: someone spray painted crude dick pictures and four-letter words on the front of a community center. Probably just some stupid kids with nothing better to do. The other one, though, was more serious. Someone broke into the local hardware store through the back, and made off with a bunch of expensive tools and other shit. They smashed the place up pretty good too, from what I understand.

"Who's talked to Sunderland's Hardware?" Angel asks.

"I'm going there this afternoon," Tweak says. "Hank says they have cameras set up back there. Hoping I can take a look at what they got."

"All right. Anyone else?" Rock looks around the table. "No? Okay. Let's talk prospects. Before we move to a vote on Bullet and Lug Nut, who's got some new names? Men you think have what it takes to be a Lord of Carnage?"

Five of the brothers speak up and tell us who they'd like to bring in. One's Striker's cousin. One's a guy Skid knows from when he lived in Tennessee. All of them sound like they've got potential, and Rock gives his okay to bring them in and have them start hanging around the club.

Finally, we get to the business of patching in two of our long-term prospects, Bullet and Lug Nut. They've both been around the club for a couple of years, and prospecting for just over a year. We talk about them one by one, going around the table and giving our arguments for and against bringing them into the Lords of Carnage. This is serious business, one of the most important decisions we can make as a club. To bring in someone new, it's crucial that every single one of us has absolute confidence and trust in him. We need to know every Lord has our back, and would fight to the death to defend our club and any one of our brothers. The Lords of Carnage is more than a club. It's a brotherhood. Anyone who doesn't understand the full weight of the vow they're taking when they're patched in doesn't deserve to wear our cut or our colors. And anyone who betrays the oath once they've taken it should expect justice to be swift, absolute, and brutal.

In the cases of Bullet and Lug Nut, I don't have a doubt in my mind about voting either one of them in. Neither do the other brothers, apparently, because they get in unanimously with almost no discussion.

Geno's about to get up and go get them, to congratulate them and bring them into the chapel, when Rock stops him.

"Hold off a few minutes," he says. "I want to tell you men about the talk I had with Oz."

We listen in silence as Rock tells us how he met with Oz at a neutral location a couple of days ago. Oz told him that the Death Devils haven't been seeing the same kinds of increases in crime and break-ins in their territory that we have. However, Oz agreed with Rock that if the Iron Spiders have the Lords of Carnage in their sights — especially if their aim is to eventually destroy us and take over our territory — the Devils could be next.

"Oz says he's open to an alliance with us," Rock concludes.

"What kind of alliance would that be?" Thorn asks.

"We didn't hammer out all the details yet," Rock answers. "He's going back to his men, to talk to them about it. He'll be contacting me soon to agree on terms."

For the first time, Geno speaks up. "Shouldn't that be something that happens with some of our brothers there? Our officers?" Rock looks at him sharply, but doesn't say anything. Geno meets his gaze evenly.

Thorn nods. "It should. I'd like to see Angel and Ghost there, at least. Maybe Brick and Geno as well."

The silence is deafening for five seconds that feel like five hours. I can feel some of the brothers tense, and I know we're all wondering if Rock will take this as a challenge to his authority.

Our president's face is dark, unmoving. Finally, his eyes roam the room, taking each of us in.

"The rest of you feel that way, too?" The question feels just short of a threat.

I glance quickly at Angel, but his face tells me he's not going to weigh in on this one.

"It's a show of strength to have your men with you," Gunner tells him. "A show of unity. I think it's a good idea."

Rock considers this. "All right," he finally says. "Angel, Ghost, and Brick." If Geno notices he's been left out, he doesn't show it. "I'll let you know when the meet's set up."

The three of us nod our assent.

"All in favor?" Rock announces. Around the table, hands raise. It's unanimous. I feel myself relax just a little bit, glad to have gotten through that moment without a showdown.

"Okay, now that that's settled, what do you say we bring in Bullet and Lug Nut?" Geno suggests, half-rising. "They're probably pissing themselves waiting by now."

"Nah, let me do it," Gunner springs up. A few of us chuckle knowingly. Gunner's always trying to fuck with people, and this is sure to be no exception.

A couple seconds later, he comes back in with Bullet. "I thought it would be better to bring them in separately," he announces to us in a low, somber voice as he closes the door. Taking his lead, the rest of us nod and do our best to look serious.

Bullet glances around the room, taking it all in. Like any prospect, he's never been in the chapel before. He looks appropriately humbled, and stands before us, back straight, hands clasped behind him.

"Prospect," Rock rumbles, "We just took our vote. And a lot of the brothers supported you." He pauses. "But as you know, a vote to patch in a prospective member has to be unanimous."

Bullet's face crumples just slightly, but he squares his chin and looks Rock in the eye.

"I understand," he says, and nods once. "I'm sorry to hear that. Is… is there any chance of a re-vote, further down the line, or is this it?"

Angel snorts and leans back. "Not sure why you'd want a re-vote, brother, since this one got you in."

Bullet blinks, and looks at Angel. It's obvious he's trying to keep his face completely neutral. "You mean…"

"Goddamnit, Angel," Gunner complains. "You suck at letting people twist in the wind."

"That's right, brother," Rock smirks. "You're in. Repeat after me. "I, Bullet Lamarr, do solemnly swear…"

Bullet recites his oath half in a daze. When he finishes, Gunner barks, "Okay, brother, now sit the fuck down. The rest of you fuckers, try to do a better job with Lug Nut than you did with Bullet."

Lug Nut comes in, we fuck with his head for as long as we can manage it, and eventually put him out of his misery. He's laughing like hell by the end of it, and he raises his hand and takes the oath, while the rest of us look on, each of us no doubt remembering the day when we were patched in ourselves. It's a solemn but happy moment, one I remember like it was yesterday.

But the solemnity doesn't last long. Once Lug Nut's been patched in, Rock bangs the gavel and the meeting's over. The brothers go over to the new patches one by one, clapping them on the back or shaking their hands. Laughter resounds through the room.

"Congratulations, brother," I say to each of them, giving them a hand shake and a nod.

"Thanks, brother," Bullet grins back. "Shit, it feels good to say that. I'm not gonna lie, I'm glad prospecting is over."

"Yeah," Gunner jokes, "maybe now the club girls will give you the time of day."

Lug Nut looks like Gunner just told him he's won the lottery. "Excuse me, gentlemen," he murmurs. "I think I'm gonna go test that theory right now."

Then someone opens the door, and we all file out toward the bar, where the party of the year is already brewing. It's gonna be a night to remember.

18
SYDNEY

I spend the next few hours in a post-coital haze, so blissed out that I'm almost sure my customers can tell I recently spent twenty minutes in my back office having what has *got* to be the best sex of my entire life. The only way I could feel more conspicuous is if I literally had on a T-shirt that had "I just had two mind-blowing orgasms!" emblazoned on the front.

My good mood continues most of the afternoon, and into the evening. It's so obvious that even Hailey notices as soon as she comes in for her closing shift.

"You're really happy today," she remarks. "What's up with you?"

"Oh, nothing," I say with a shrug. "It's just a nice day out, so I'm in a good mood."

Hailey stops what she's doing and cocks her head at me. "Are you serious?" she asks, her hands on her hips. I turn toward the front window.

It's raining. I hadn't noticed.

"I mean, we need the rain," I say hastily. "So that's nice, right?"

Hailey purses her lips. "You're full of shit," she says bluntly. "Something's happened. And you're not telling me."

"I'm your boss, young lady. I have no obligation to tell you a thing."

"Oh, my God, something *did* happen!" She's triumphant. "Something happened with the hot biker guy! Am I right? I'm right, aren't I?"

Dammit. I'd been hoping to avoid the subject of Brick with Hailey, especially since the night he came to the shop and I told her to leave. I should have known it would be impossible. Like most teen girls, she loves gossip, especially about the male of the species.

"Nothing happened!" I exclaim, rolling my eyes. My dad raised me to have a good poker face, but I can tell I'm not fooling Hailey for a minute.

"Oh, come on! Tell me! I promise I won't tell another soul." She gives me such a serious, earnest look that I almost burst out laughing.

"Hailey. Listen to me," I repeat. "Nothing. Happened."

"Fine. Be a killjoy," she sighs with a toss of her lavender ponytail. "I'll just use my imagination."

Hailey fake-pouts for the rest of the shift, and I let her. I'm not about to give in, so she can just live with it. Tonight's the last night I'm helping her close the shop before she tries doing it by herself. As eight o'clock nears, I can't help but sneak glances out the window, wondering whether Gavin will show up. Even though my pulse begins to race at the thought, I know I'll *never* get Hailey off my back if he does.

In the end, he doesn't come by. I'm both relieved and disappointed. Hailey's mom comes to pick her up, and I lock the shop and go out the back. Even though Gavin isn't here, I guess his badgering at me to be careful has had an effect on me, because I notice I'm ultra-cautious and aware of my surroundings as I go to my car and lock myself in.

I'm driving back to my place when my phone buzzes in my purse, telling me I have a text. My stomach does a little flip of excitement, even though I know it can't be him. He doesn't have my phone number, and I don't have his.

The euphoric cloud I've been floating on for the past few hours dips a little as I remember that Gavin and I are basically nothing to each other. His weird preoccupation with the security level of my coffee shop notwithstanding, we're more or less strangers. *And that's fine,* I tell myself emphatically. *You don't need him to be your boyfriend. In fact, you don't even* want *a boyfriend, remember?*

When I get home and turn off my car, it's as if the fates had taken it upon themselves to remind me exactly *why* I don't want a boyfriend. I pull out my phone to discover that the text I got is from Devon.

U will b fuckin sorry u whore better watch urslef i know wehre u live

I have to sit in my locked car and force myself to breathe deeply and evenly. My hands clutching the steering wheel so tightly my knuckles are white. *He found my new number,* my brain repeats crazily. *He found my new number.* He's not letting this go.

When I manage to get my breathing under control, I flick my eyes briefly back to my phone again, and then grip my keys with my pepper spray tightly in my hand. My house looks undisturbed, all the lights off except the one on my front porch.

I try to talk myself out of the prickles of fear tingling on the back of my neck. From the mistakes in the text, it looks like he might have been drinking, or maybe even on something stronger. So maybe he's just drunk and lashing out at me to make himself feel better. Besides, as I've told myself before, if he really was coming after me, why would he tell me about it? Why wouldn't he want to take me by surprise? It doesn't make sense.

He just doesn't like losing. He's just doing this as a display of power so he can feel like a big man. That's all it is. He's mad, but he wouldn't hurt me.

That's what I tell myself, anyway.

I have to admit, though, it makes me feel a whole lot safer to have all the security stuff Gavin installed at the coffee shop. Not that I'd tell him that, of course. I smile in spite of myself, instinctively knowing that he'd never let me live it down if I did.

Like the first time, I don't respond to Devon's text. I can't see the point. Instead, I toss my phone on the couch and double-check that my door is locked and dead-bolted. Then I do a nerve-wracking check of the entire house to make sure no one's here, tell myself off for being such a ninny, and go in the bathroom to take a long, hot shower.

When I come out, wrapped in a fluffy bathrobe, I see that my screen is lit up with another text. My stomach lurches sickeningly at the thought that Devon's messaged me again, but I force myself to pick up the phone and read what it says.

Missed you at the coffee shop tonight.

A dizzying rush of adrenaline spikes through my system, making me feel like I might throw up. *Shit! Devon's here in Tanner Springs? He knows where the shop is?* My mind races frantically — trying to think what I should do, what I should say — when I realize with a start that the text is all alone on the screen.

And that the area code is for Tanner Springs, not New Jersey.

Weakly, I slump down on the couch and actually start laughing with relief.

I text back:

> You can't come there every single night to guard me and escort me home, you know.

A couple of seconds later comes the response:

> Wanna bet?

I'm trying to think of a smartass reply when Gavin sends me another message:

> So, you're not dead, which is positive. You make it home safe?

Yes, I'm fine. How did you get my phone number?

I'm a man of mystery.

Apparently.

For some reason, I'm grinning like an idiot as I watch the little dots dance on the screen, telling me he's typing.

I've got some shit going on tonight, but I'll stop by the shop tomorrow. I have a present for you.

I risk a reference to earlier today:

Is it as romantic as a security camera?

A second later he replies:

Babe, you have no idea. See you tomorrow.

I just barely hold myself back from typing a response to him, because I know it will probably come out all super-dorky and overly attached and just plain *uncool.* Instead, I tell myself that leaving it like that will make me seem casual and self-assured and not reading too much into any of this.

144

Which is what I *desperately* want to be.

The sex this afternoon in my office with Gavin was absolutely *incredible*, so much so that I would pretty much do anything short of murder to do it again. And I'm really, *really* hoping we do. But I also don't want to let myself start overthinking it. He's not exactly someone who screams "boyfriend material," after all. If anything, he's probably the kind of guy that probably has mind-melting sex with random women most days of the week.

Thinking this now, I have to ignore a little flush of disappointment. Maybe he just thinks of me as… I dunno, an easy lay, or something. *Stop that, Syd. Don't be stupidly sexist. You're both consenting adults. He wanted it, you wanted it, so it happened. End of story.*

And that's true, right? It seems like maybe he wants to continue whatever this thing is, and even that he likes me enough to find out my number somehow and apparently to bring me a present tomorrow. I should just be happy with that, and be happy that for at least a little while it looks like I'm gonna be having amazing sex. Where's the downside in that?

Armed with this incredibly air-tight logic, I decide to make an early night of it and get to the shop bright and early tomorrow. I pull my still-damp hair into a high ponytail and put it in a loose braid, smiling to myself. Soon, though, my thoughts wander back to Devon. In all the excitement of flirting with Gavin, I'd almost forgotten about him for a few minutes.

He said he knows where I live.

Could he be serious? Could he really be thinking about coming here?

I try to tell myself again that there's probably no reason to be worried. I mean, yes, it is a little concerning that he's sending me menacing messages. Devon and I didn't exactly part on the best of terms. But it still seems like an overreaction to think they're anything more than empty threats. After all, the money I took (*my money*, I remind myself fiercely) was chicken feed compared to the kind of cash he usually deals in. I don't know why he'd bother following me to try to get it back, when logically it's not worth the time he'd be away from Atlantic City.

All this time that I've been going back and forth in my mind about Devon, there's a tiny voice in my head that keeps growing louder. I've been pushing it away, but it's clamoring to be heard, and finally I can't ignore it anymore.

You know what Devon wanted from you went far beyond just the money you could make him. You know he doesn't let go easily of what he thinks of as his.

I shiver, and pull my bathrobe more tightly around me.

That may be true. Maybe I underestimated how attached Devon was to me romantically. Our affair was never something I thought of as permanent. I just assumed he felt the same. Or maybe I just *hoped* that was how he felt. If I'm completely honest with myself, sometimes Devon's proprietary attitude toward me veered toward the controlling, especially when he thought one of the other men on our team was getting too friendly with me.

Still, it seems crazy that he would come all the way here to hurt me. I can't have been *that* important to him. And besides, in all the time I knew Devon, he was never *violent* toward me.

No, a little voice in my head says. *But he was violent toward other people. Particularly when he felt like he had something to prove.*

It's true. The only times I ever saw Devon hurt someone was when he was cornered. When he's in serious trouble, he reacts like a caged animal. Unpredictable and dangerous.

A little cold knot takes root in my stomach.

Has something happened? What has Devon gotten himself into?

And is he really coming for me?

19
BRICK

The party we have to celebrate patching in Bullet and Lug Nut is a fucking blowout, so much so that I don't drag my ass up to my apartment at the clubhouse to get some sleep until close to four a.m. But I still manage to pull myself out of bed the next morning and head over to the Golden Cup with my present for Sydney.

When I get to the coffee shop, she's just serving an older lady with round glasses and silver hair holding a thick book. Sydney looks up as I come in and gives me a tiny smile of recognition as she rings up the lady's coffee. I walk up to the counter, my hands behind my back.

Sydney looks a little tired again today, but it does nothing to make her any less gorgeous or sexy. She's wearing a little pink tank top that brings out the fullness of her lips and the creaminess of her skin. I briefly contemplate taking her in the back for a repeat of yesterday, but I'm pretty sure she wouldn't agree to it with people in the shop.

"Morning, babe," I growl. "You're looking good enough to eat."

I'm rewarded with a blush. "Is that my present?" she asks, nodding toward my back.

"It is," I nod, and pull it out.

"A fire extinguisher!" she marvels, clapping her hands together. "You shouldn't have!"

I laugh and go into the back to get to work installing the thing. I remove the old extinguisher from the wall, then install the new one in its place. The whole thing only takes me a couple minutes. While I'm working, Sydney comes back to join me.

"It's just what I always wanted," she smirks. "How did you know?"

"I know how to treat a woman right," I tell her.

"You do," she agrees. "Much more romantic than flowers or candy. But how do I know you're not just trying to get me into bed?"

"I *am* trying to get you into bed," I growl, and catch her by the waist. "Or at least back into the office."

"Is that so?" she asks, a challenge in her voice.

"It sure as hell is." I pull her toward me, a little roughly. She lifts her head and looks at me, her eyes wide, pupils large.

"And what if I say no?" she says a little breathlessly.

"Then I let you go," I murmur, and dip my mouth toward hers. "But you won't."

My lips cover hers. Sydney moans into my mouth as her body melts into mine. I kiss her hungrily, my cock hardening. Her arms wind around my neck, heat growing between us. I push her against the counter, and my hands move down to cup her ass and pull her against me. She whimpers and arches toward me, angling her hips so that her softness is against my hardness.

"Fuck, Sydney," I rasp. "Let's take this in the back."

"Hello?" an impatient voice calls out just then. "Can I get some service out here?"

"Oh, for fuck's sake." Sydney breaks away from me. "It's kolache guy."

"Oh, brother," I mutter under my breath, remembering the old guy who's never happy with anything.

Sydney slides down from the counter and adjusts her clothing. "I better go serve him," she murmurs. She looks up at me conspiratorially. "I actually *have* kolaches today. He might just faint from surprise."

She slips away from me, and I let her go. I finish screwing the extinguisher housing to the wall, making sure it's secure — which has the added benefit of giving me time to calm the raging hard-on in my pants. I walk out into the shop just as Sydney is offering the old guy a kolache.

"They look close enough," he's saying skeptically, peering into the pastry case with a suspicious frown. "But that doesn't mean anything."

Behind him, the older lady with the round tortoise-shell glasses and the silver bob has come up for a refill. When she sees what he's looking at, she opens her eyes wide.

"Oh, I haven't had a kolache in years!" she exclaims. "Not since I was a girl growing up in Cedar Rapids, Iowa."

"Would you two like to sample one?" Sydney offers graciously. I can't help but smile at her charm offensive. It's a smart move. Who can turn down a free pastry?

Sydney takes a kolache with cream cheese filling out of the case and cuts it in half. She places each half on a separate plate and slides them toward the man and the woman. The woman picks hers up first, and takes an experimental bite.

"Is it any good?" The man sniffs.

"It's perfect," the woman says with a satisfied smile. "Exactly the way it should taste. My goodness, that brings back memories."

The man picks his half up and takes a taste. Sydney watches as he chews and swallows.

"I always say, a bakery isn't worth much unless they have kolaches," he tells the woman. He doesn't remark one way or another on the pastry, but his voice softens just a touch. "I grew up near Columbus. Bakeries there — the real ones, not the high-falutin' *modern* ones — have some of the best kolaches." He pauses a beat. "This one's pretty good," he admits grudgingly.

"Thank you," Sydney says soberly. "I'll keep trying."

The man orders a coffee and takes the plate with his half of the kolache over to the table where his friends are. Sydney refills the woman's espresso drink and she goes back to her book. When they're both taken care of, she turns to me and does a tiny fist-pump of victory.

"He liked it!" she exults. "I can't believe he didn't just spit it out like I was feeding him rat poison!"

"Good thing, too," I grin. "That was a hell of a lot of effort you went through to win over one customer."

"I can't help it," she smiles back. "Sometimes I just get an idea in my head and I can't let go of it. I like a challenge."

"So do I," I murmur, moving just a little closer to her.

She cocks her head. "Are you calling me a challenge?"

"You do take a little more work than I'm used to."

Her smile fades. "I didn't ask you for anything, you know."

"Hey." I reach up and brush a strand of hair back from her face. "Joke."

She relaxes just a little. "Okay."

The bell to the door tinkles. I glance back to see a group of women coming into the cafe. "So, are you working all day today?"

"No, actually. Hailey has the day off from school today. Some sort of teacher in-service thing. So I'm done at three, and she's going to close tonight."

"Where do you live? I'll pick you up at your place tonight around seven."

"'Do you happen to be free tonight, Sydney?'" she recites in a pointed tone. "'If you are, I was wondering if you wanted to go do something.'"

"You're free," I growl, leaning in close enough that I can smell her shampoo. "What's your address?"

"I should turn you down, you know." Her breath hitches in her throat. "Just for being an ass."

"I'll make it up to you." I reach down and slide my hand in between her skin and the waistband of her jeans. Keeping the thin fabric of her panties between us, I graze a finger softly against her clit. She gasps and shudders.

"Three twenty-seven Adams," she whispers.

"Don't dress up," I say thickly. "You might not be wearing anything for long."

20
SYDNEY

It probably sounds unbelievable, but in all the months I've been in Tanner Springs, I've never had a single visitor inside my house.

What can I say? I work morning, noon and night. I very literally do not have a life outside of the coffee shop.

For the most part, it's not something that bothers me much. I like what I do. And back in Atlantic City, my social life was pretty non-existent as well. Like everyone else in my old circle, I followed the bizarre, anti-circadian rhythms of the professional gambling universe. I slept when I could, ate whatever was on hand, and spent most of my time in the windowless expanses of any number of casinos.

The nature of the life I led meant that I wasn't exactly meeting lots of new people and throwing dinner parties or anything. Outsiders weren't to be trusted. Hell, insiders were barely to be trusted. And when I had a rare moment to

myself, usually all I wanted to do was hole up and lose myself
in a book, or lock the door and fall into a luxurious,
dreamless sleep until I woke up without an alarm.

So, to say I'm not used to having "friends" as such is an
understatement. Beyond the mostly superficial conversations
I have at the coffee shop, the most interaction I typically have
on any given day is with the checkout lady at the grocery
store or the occasional gas station attendant.

When I get home from the Golden Cup around three-
thirty, I'm already having a mild panic attack at the realization
that Gavin will be here in just a few short hours. I look
around the tiny house I've been renting with a critical frown,
trying to view it like someone seeing it for the first time. It
has the look of someone who's just moving in: no pictures or
art work on the wall, no knick-knacks or sentimental objects
anywhere. Just a generic, L-shaped chocolate-colored
sectional couch, a glass coffee table, and a flat screen TV
sitting on a low, dark wood stand that I got at a second hand
store. The only colorful thing in the room is a chevron-
patterned rug that I bought on impulse one day in a desperate
attempt to make the room look less sterile.

My bedroom isn't much better. The queen sized bed has
practically never been made, the gray and white comforter
twisted into a ball with the sheets in the middle of the
mattress.

It's not exactly like Gavin is an interior designer or
anything. But knowing that he'll be here soon and will see all
this makes me feel self-conscious, all the same. I do a hurried

vacuum of the place, make the bed, and manage to dig up a couple pictures I've been meaning to hang since I moved in. A couple of hours later, and at least the place doesn't look quite so sad and pathetic. Satisfied there's not much more I can do, I take a quick shower, dry my hair, and put on a little bit of makeup. I pull on a clean pair of jeans and my favorite fitted top, and try to ignore the heat that pools between my legs when I remember what he said about not wearing my clothes for very long.

Finally, when I can't think of anything else to do, I pour myself a glass of wine and sit down on the couch with a book and some music, and try not to lose my mind until he gets here.

Eventually, around a quarter to seven, I hear the far-off but familiar rumble of a Harley. I stand up quickly, almost spilling my wine all over my shirt, and take a few deep breaths. I don't know why I'm so nervous, but I feel like my heart's going to beat out of my chest. Through the front window, I see Gavin pull up in front of my house. I open the front door and go out to meet him as he cuts the engine and slides off the bike.

"Babe," he rumbles, crossing the distance between us in just a couple of steps. "You look good enough to eat."

He's wearing his leather, of course, and his face is even more tanned than usual, as though he's been out in the sun today. "You look pretty good, too," I risk. My bottom lip slides nervously between my teeth.

"You bite that lip like that, I'm gonna have to take you inside and bite it for you," he murmurs, pulling me close.

"Is that what you had in mind?" I half-gasp as his lips heat up my skin. I feel kind of *melty* — like he's turning me boneless.

"I had in mind to take you out on my bike." He growls against my ear. "But I think that's gonna have to wait. I'm not gonna be able to ride like this." His thick, hard heat presses against me, making me shiver. I'm instantly wet, embarrassingly so. A low throb begins between my legs that makes it suddenly hard to think.

"We… we could go inside," I say, my voice trembling.

Almost before the words are out of my mouth he's picked me up and is carrying me toward the house. I half-think to be embarrassed, in case one of my neighbors is outside and can see us, but being in his arms is making me feel sort of dizzy. I wrap my arms around his neck as he yanks open my front door and carries me through it. Inside, he doesn't even slow down. "Bedroom," he orders.

"Down the hall, on the right," I breathe. Already my pulse is racing. It's amazing how quickly I just abandon myself to him. I don't think I could resist him no matter what the price. I wouldn't know how.

In the bedroom, he slides me from his arms and puts me on the bed. For a second, I silently curse myself for not changing the sheets this afternoon. He steps back and unzips his pants, pushing his jeans down until they hang to his thighs. He takes out his cock and wraps his hand around the base. It's the first time I've really gotten a good look at it, and oh, my God, it's massive. No wonder he felt so good inside me last time. I suppress a moan as I feel the throbbing between my legs grow.

"You know what I want," he says huskily as he strokes. "Take off your jeans."

I do as I'm told, sliding my jeans off and kicking them to the floor.

"Take off your shirt and bra."

My eyes locked on his, I pull the shirt over my head and unclasp the bra. When I'm naked except for my panties, his eyes slide slowly down my body with unconcealed lust. His gaze lingers on my breasts; my nipples grow taut.

"Touch yourself."

I open my mouth to protest, but I know he won't take no for an answer. I've never done this in front of anyone. My cheeks flame red as my fingers slide under the fabric of my panties.

"Push the panties aside," he commands. I slide one finger into my wet opening, and slide the juices against my throbbing clit. It feels so good that I gasp and half-close my eyes.

"Fuck, yes," he growls. He's stroking himself slowly, from root to tip. I reach out for him, my fingers circling him near the top, loving the heat and hardness of him. He groans at my touch, a bead of pre-cum appearing at the tip. My mouth actually waters at the thought of tasting him, feeling the velvet of his skin against my tongue.

"I want to taste you," I say. I didn't know I was going to say the words, I couldn't stop them before they came out of my mouth.

"Not yet. Not tonight."

He moves his hand and cups my face as I begin to stroke, in the same rhythm that I'm teasing myself. I turn and wrap my lips around the tip of his finger, sucking it into my mouth and moaning as I imagine it's his cock. "Fuck, Sydney," he groans as my tongue swirls around, showing him what I want to do to him. In my hand, I feel his cock pulse and jump. He pulls away from me and takes a step back.

By now, my whole body is crying out for his touch. I whimper and stroke my clit, faster, faster, my whole body aching with need. He knows it, too, I can tell by the feral half-smile on his face as he slows down his own rhythm as mine speeds up.

"Tell me what you want me to do to you," he rasps. I can see it in his eyes, he won't give me what I need until I ask for it.

"I want you to fuck me," I whisper. "I need to come."

"Take off your panties," he says. "Spread your legs for me."

I slide them down my legs and pull them off. Hesitating just a moment, I open my thighs slowly. He waits. I open them wider, until I'm completely exposed.

"Jesus fucking Christ, that's gorgeous," he says, his voice thick. He reaches into his pocket and pulls out a condom. Stepping out of his jeans, he slides it over his shaft and lowers himself onto the bed between my legs. "You're so fucking wet for me, Sydney. God damn, you're so wet."

He slicks the head of his cock through my wetness. I half-cry out, my head falling back as I arch my hips toward him. Just seconds more like that and I'm going to come, and I want it, I *need* it so badly.

"Please make me come," I beg him.

"What do you want, Sydney? Tell me what you want."

"I want… your cock," I pant. "I want your cock inside me."

His hands are on my hips then, lifting me upright and off the bed so that I'm straddling him. He guides me down onto his shaft, the top of his cock sliding deliciously against my clit as my pussy opens and stretches to take him all in. The heat of him alone almost sends me over the edge.

"Sydney, Jesus fuck, do you feel what you do to me?" he mutters against my throat, his voice thick. I can feel the pulse of my heartbeat thrumming against his lips. "All I can think about for weeks is how badly I want to be inside you. I'm going to fuck you within an inch of your life, and you're going to come around my cock. I want to watch you lose control, because it's the most gorgeous thing I've ever seen."

I wrap my arms around his neck and cling to him as he begins to thrust deep inside me, his cock wet and slick with my juices. It's better than anything I could imagine as my hips move with his, sending me higher and higher.

"This is what you wanted," he urges me.

"Yes, Gavin," I whimper, digging my nails into his back as my thighs tighten around him. My eyes begin to flutter closed.

"Look at me, Sydney," he commands. My eyes snap open to lock on his. It's impossibly intimate, like he's looking into my soul. I do as he tells me, as my breathing grows shallow and ragged. I'm so close, so close, and then it's here, he's here with me fucking me and it's so good and any second I'm…

"Oh, God, I'm going to…" I gasp, and then my body convulses as my orgasm rips through me. He covers my mouth with his, swallowing my cries as the waves hit me, and then all his muscles clench at once and he groans and lets go, coming inside me in one explosive thrust.

We stay like that, him buried inside me, kissing deep and desperate, gasping for air but unable to stop. Eventually, the racing of my heart begins to slow, and the sheen of sweat that covers me starts to cool. Gavin's hand leaves my back and travels upward to my face. Gently, he brushes my tangled hair away from my face, then grazes a callused thumb along my cheek.

He doesn't say anything.

Neither do I.

21
BRICK

"So, have I earned the *real* story of what brought you here
to Tanner Springs?" I ask her.

We're lying in bed, covers pulled over us. Sydney is
nestled in the crook of my arm.

I'm fighting a wave of something I don't quite
understand. What just happened between the two of us, just
now... it wasn't like anything I've ever experienced with any
woman.

I've had plenty of sex. I've had more women than I could
ever count. Half of them, I didn't even know their names at
the time, or if I did I forgot them as soon as I pulled out.

When I felt Sydney clench around me, her orgasm felt
almost like it became a part of mine. We came together, with

her shuddering in my arms. It made me feel like a million goddamn bucks.

Even worse, it made me want to shut out the rest of the world and just stay here with her. Doing nothing but this. And maybe occasionally ordering a pizza so we don't starve to death.

For the first time, I think I understand how a man could fall down a rabbit hole for a woman. The soft cascade of her hair against my chest, the sounds she makes when I move inside her, the way she holds onto me for dear life as she starts to come… all of it is making its way into the pathways of my mind. Threatening to stick there. To make her something — someone — I don't want to be without.

I want to know more about Sydney Banner. I want to know things no one else knows about her.

And as good as it feels to be with her, alarm bells are starting to sound in my brain.

As a Marine, I got used to deprivation. To testing the limits of my physical and emotional endurance. I got used to doing without, to living a life stripped bare of anything but training, readiness, and being constantly alert to danger. That was the part I ended up liking best about it, strangely enough. There was no time or energy to waste thinking about shit that didn't matter. The past was over and done with. The future was something that might never even happen.

When I got out of the Corps, patching into the Lords of Carnage gave me something similar. There was a lot more partying, and a lot more pussy. But the basic premise was the same, at least for me. My role as a member, and eventually as the Enforcer, was clear. Unlike some of the brothers, I didn't have any family to speak of. No old lady, no kids, nothing to be except a Lord. When I see Ghost with Jenna and their kids, or Hawk with Samantha, I tell myself I'm happy for them, but that kind of life is not for me. I'm not a man who's interested in constructing a future, with a family and all that shit. All I want is my club, and my lake house, and to be left alone.

That's what I tell myself.

Which is why, instead of lying here asking Sydney about her childhood, I should be pulling on my pants and getting the hell out of here.

"What do you mean, the 'real story'?" she asks with a yawn, and throws an arm across my chest.

"You said you grew up in Atlantic City, and that your dad is in the 'resort and casino business'," I remind her.

"*Was* in the business," she corrects me. "He's dead."

"Oh." I don't say anything for a moment. The way she says this — *He's dead* — is so matter of fact. She's sure as hell not asking for sympathy from me. But there's a tightness in her voice, just barely perceptible, that tells me she's working hard to hide the pain from me. And maybe from herself.

After a beat, I decide to push a little, "Do you miss him?"

I can feel her stop breathing for just a moment. "Yeah."

And then I decide.

"Tell me about him."

Sydney pauses, making me think she's about to change the subject. But then she doesn't. "He wasn't the most conventional dad in the world, but he loved me," she begins. "And my mom wasn't in the picture. She left my dad when I was four. And I have no idea where she is today, or if she's even alive. My dad told me she never really wanted to be a mom. So, he was kind of all I had."

"Shit." I pull her closer. "So, he was a gambler, huh?"

She chuckles softly. "You figured that out, did you?"

"Yeah. I have uncanny powers of perception."

"He was born in North Carolina," she murmurs. "I think he was a high school dropout. Came to New Jersey when he was eighteen or so. Met my mom, dazzled her with his charm and good looks, and got her pregnant before either one of them really knew what was happening. Hence, me."

"Lucky me," I murmur against her hair, before I can stop myself.

It feels like something in the air shifts. My heart pounds in my chest. If she notices it, she doesn't say anything.

"Like I said, my mom left when I was young," she continues, as if I haven't spoken. "I don't have any memory of her. So, it was just the two of us. My dad moved us around a lot. I'd go to school sometimes, sometimes not. Every once in a while, he'd come into some good money and we'd put down some roots for a while. But it seemed like just when I'd start really get attached to one place, make some real friends, he'd say it was time to go. So after a while, I didn't bother making friends so much.

"My dad loved me, though," she says in a small, sad voice. "I mean, in his own way. He wasn't really equipped to be a normal father, but he did the best he could by me. He felt bad, I think, about hauling me all over the place, so he'd buy me books and stuff and try to make sure I was reading them instead of rotting my brain watching TV or playing video games all the time. He'd talk to me about gambling, too. It was what he knew, you know? Something he could teach me himself. I don't think he really intended to make a gambler out of me, exactly. It seemed more like he thought he was teaching me about the world through the lessons he gave me. About human weaknesses, and how to read people, and how to understand whether the odds are against you or not."

Listening to Sydney talk about her father, I can't help but picture her as a young girl. Red hair in a tangle, always the new girl in a new school. Raised to fend for herself. My throat constricts a little. I resist the urge to hold her tighter, not wanting to distract her from telling her story.

"When I was old enough, Dad started teaching me the tricks of his trade," she tells me. "I was most interested in blackjack, so he taught me how to count cards. At first, it was mostly just a math exercise. But it turned out I was good at it. I wasn't doing it at the casinos, of course, since I wasn't old enough. And my dad absolutely forbid me to gamble for money before I turned eighteen. But when I did turn eighteen, I started testing out what I'd learned by reading and doing simulations online. Eventually, he got me into the gambling circuit by getting me fake identification saying I was twenty-one, so I could get into the casinos." She laughs softly. "Turns out that my irregular schooling helped on that front. I didn't have a high school diploma, so it was harder to prove I wasn't as old as I said I was.

"At first, I just watched the other people, and made sure I broke even so I didn't arouse suspicion. Then, eventually, I started letting myself win a little more often. I'd set limits to how much I'd allow myself to make, to discipline myself."

I think back to when I first started coming into the Golden Cup. How it always seemed to me that Sydney had the look of someone who had learned how to fend for herself early. I'm starting to get why she chafes so much when she thinks I'm treating her like she's helpless.

I also know, instinctively, that if she thinks I'm feeling sorry for her now, she'll shut down and stop talking.

"This isn't exactly the life story I'd expect from a small town coffee shop owner," I tease, keeping my voice light.

"No, I suppose not." She raises her head and gives me a playful grin. "Imagine how scandalized kolache guy would be if he knew."

"So, you were good at it," I prompt. "Gambling."

"I was," she nods.

"That how you made enough money to start up the coffee shop?"

"Eventually, yeah. It's a little more complicated than that, though."

Sydney pauses for a moment, like she's considering how much further to go with her story.

"I wasn't planning on making a living out of it. And even though my dad taught me as much as he could about the tricks of his trade, he didn't want me to be a professional gambler, either. He always told me it was a dangerous life, an uncertain and unstable one. And of course I knew that, just from the way I was raised. I wanted to go to college, actually." She sighs. "I dreamed of having a normal life, of living in a dorm and eating pizza and ramen, and study sessions, and having a roommate, and girlfriends..." Sydney trails off and gives a dry little laugh. "Well. That didn't happen. A couple months after my eighteenth birthday, my dad started coughing a ton. We thought it was bronchitis, but the meds the doc gave him didn't work. Finally, he went in for some more tests to see what was up. Turned out he had lung cancer. By the time they caught it, he was almost at stage four. He was dead six weeks later."

"Holy shit, Sydney. I'm sorry." I feel like a jackass for saying something so trite, but it's true. I'm sorry as hell for her, losing basically the only person she had at such a young age. It's true, I walked away from my last shitty foster home at around the same time, but at least I *chose* it. And besides, the home I left was no kind of home at all. Sydney at least had a parent who loved her, and it's clear how much she loved him. Looking at her face now, I see all the pain etched on it that she's hidden from the world.

"Thanks," she says simply. "Life is shitty sometimes. If it's one thing my father taught me, it's that the odds are always against you. You do everything you can to beat them, but…" She shrugs. "Eventually, the table always wins."

I wish I could tell her that's not true, but the words freeze in my throat. I'm not exactly a rainbows and unicorns kind of guy, and she's not stupid. She'd smell the bullshit from a mile away.

A lump forms in my throat where the words would be. If I had any to offer.

22
BRICK

"After Dad died, I had to figure out a way to make a living." Sydney has propped herself up on one elbow. Her eyes don't quite meet mine as she continues to talk, and it's almost as though she's telling someone else's story, her voice devoid of emotion.

"He had been on a losing streak when he got sick, and the medical bills wiped out all his savings," she continues. "So, I did what I knew how to do: I started making the rounds of the casinos, playing just enough to make ends meet, and keeping a low enough profile so no one would get wise to me. Counting cards isn't illegal, but casinos don't like it, for obvious reasons. I was lucky I was a girl, and young enough that most people just assumed I was some college kid on vacation or something. As long as I was careful, and didn't call attention to myself, I managed to stay under the radar for the most part." She hesitates for a moment. "But eventually, one of my dad's gambling associates recognized me one day and had me watched to see how good I was. The people who were watching me noticed I was counting, saw my potential, and went back to tell him. A few days later, Devon had me brought to the suite where he was staying and asked me to join his team."

"Team?" I ask, not understanding.

"Yeah." She takes a deep breath and lets it out. All of a sudden, she sounds tired. "There are teams all over the major casinos, especially in Atlantic City and Vegas. They're run like a business, with rules and perks, and incentive systems. Behind the teams are investors, too, who try to make money off a team or an individual counter." Her face grows dark for a moment, like she's remembering something she doesn't want to talk about. "I did that for a little over three years. The thing is, on a team, the money can be better, but your fate is also tied to everyone else on the team. We had months of losing from time to time. And even though I was good at it, the lifestyle just wasn't for me. I had seen what it did to my dad, and I never had the drive or the passion for winning that carried the others through."

Sydney looks at me now, almost as though she's registering that I'm still there. "In movies, they romanticize that life," she says. "But the reality is that it's grueling and intense. I thought about my dad, and how his whole existence had been focused on beating the odds, and decided I needed to get out before the life claimed me." She looks away again, her eyes dark and troubled. "So I took the money that was mine, and left town. I came here because it was the only place

I could think of that was far enough away from what I'd known."

"Your great-aunt told you about Tanner Springs," I murmur. "Right?"

"Right," she nods, looking impressed. One corner of her mouth curves up slightly. "My great-aunt Edna — she's the only relative of my dad's he was in touch with — had a high school friend who lived here. Edna's dead now, but I remember she always used to talk about visiting Tanner Springs in the summers. She loved it here. Since I had literally nowhere else to go, I figured I'd take a chance. So here I am."

"Here you are," I agree. "Atlantic City's loss is Tanner Springs' gain."

She gives me a little smirk. "At least I can be proud I've brought decent coffee to this town."

"Does anyone from your former life know you're here?" I ask, out of curiosity.

Something in Sydney's expression flickers, just for a moment. It happens so fast that I almost think I'm imagining it. But then she smiles at me, and it's different somehow. Like a part of her has closed off.

"Nope. No one," she says, a little too airily. "Don't blow my cover, okay?"

Suddenly, everything feels a little off.

I want to push it — to call her bluff and ask her what's wrong. What she's not telling me.

But I don't. Because something tells me I wouldn't get it out of her. Not right now.

And if I'm honest, it's also because selfishly, I sense it might wreck the mood.

So instead, I file it away to ask her about later.

"You're the first person I've told all that to," she murmurs, tracing a little circle on the sheet with her finger. "In Tanner Springs or anywhere."

The weight of her words hits me then, as I realize what she's saying. Sydney probably hasn't had a lot of people to confide in, given the life she's had. The fact that she felt comfortable enough to let me in — to get a glimpse of the world she worked so hard to leave behind — is a gift, something precious and fragile. It's more than I expected. I don't know quite what to do with it.

"Your secret's safe with me," I say carefully. "Thanks for telling me."

"You know, you're a surprisingly good listener," she muses, biting her lip, and then smirks at me. "For a big bad biker guy, that is."

I snort and grab her by the waist, making her squeal. "Enough talking," I growl. "I can't have you thinking I have a sensitive side. You'll ruin my goddamn reputation."

"Your secret's safe with m-*eeek*!" she shrieks as I toss her back on the bed. She starts to giggle as I lower myself on top of her, and pretends to protest, but the giggles turn to moans soon enough. I'm already hard again, and she's wet and ready for me. I push myself inside of her and we rock together, Sydney wrapping her legs around my hips and whimpering as I drive myself deeper and deeper. We come together, and then I hold her, so tightly I'm afraid I'm hurting her, but I can't let go.

* * *

"So, your turn," Sydney murmurs, her fingers tracing the scar patterns on my left hand and arm. "Tell me about this."

We haven't slept. We haven't eaten. It's still dark outside, and quiet. The sky hasn't yet shifted from inky black to just a tiny hint of gray, announcing the morning, but it will soon.

I shrug. "Not much to tell," I say, winding my fingers through hers. "It happened in the Marines." I stop for a moment, and weigh how much to tell her. It's an ugly story. Not exactly anyone's idea of pillow talk. "I was stationed in Helmand Province, Afghanistan. Some guys in my unit were hit by an RPG. Pulling one of them out to safety, I got burned pretty bad."

She looks at me, her eyes dark with sympathy. "Did you get him out?"

"Yeah," I say softly. "But it wasn't enough. He didn't survive."

I stop talking, thinking of the aftermath. Sydney seems to sense that I don't want to talk about it.

"We should get some sleep," she murmurs. "It'll be morning soon. We're both gonna be dead tired today."

"Worth it," I say, pulling her hand to my lips and kissing it.

She nods, her eyes shining. "Worth it," she whispers.

Sydney drifts off to sleep, and I listen as her breathing slows and deepens. She's right, I'm fucking tired as hell and I'm gonna feel like shit later, but I also know I'm not going to sleep. Instead, I lie there and think about the rest of the Helmand story.

About Rob Sims, the Marine I tried and failed to save that day.

About how he was always talking about his wife. How he was trying so hard to stay alive so he could make it back home to her.

"Fuck," I mutter under my breath.

Next to me, Sydney stirs and sighs, but doesn't wake up.

Sims was a hell of a Marine. He was the guy you wanted next to you in a fight: solid and dependable as they come, the guy you knew would always have your back. He was a straight fucking arrow, too.

And Jesus, he fucking loved his wife. He talked about her all the time. Her name was Tina. I can remember the picture of her Sims had as his home screen on his phone, because he'd show it to anyone and everyone who asked about her. She was dark-haired and wide-eyed, and even though the picture only showed her from the chest up, you could tell she had a hell of a body.

Sims and Tina had only been together for a year before they got married, and he shipped off to Afghanistan shortly after that. Sims worried about Tina a lot — about whether she was adjusting to her new life on a military base without him, far from her family and the friends she'd left behind. A few months before he ended up getting killed, Sims confided to me once or twice that they'd been fighting a lot, and that sometimes she wouldn't reply to his emails after an argument, or wouldn't pick up the phone when they'd agreed to Skype. He always forgave her for it, though. "She has it rougher than I do, in a lot of ways," he'd say. "She's all alone, without a lot to do on the base. It's tougher to be the one left behind."

Personally, I thought maybe it was a little tougher to be living in a hundred-degree hellhole, getting shot at and explosives lobbed at you, but I figured I'd keep that shit to myself.

A couple of months after Sims got killed, I came up for a two week leave. I hadn't originally planned to go back to the States, but at the last minute I decided I felt an obligation to go see Sims' widow and offer my condolences in person. I figured she might take some comfort in knowing something about his life as a soldier. How respected he was by his fellow Marines, and how fucking sorry we were that he was gone.

I found out Tina Sims had moved off the military base where she'd been living and into an apartment, a few miles away but still in the same town. I got hold of her address, and her phone number too. I thought about calling her to let her know I wanted to pay her a visit, but I've never been much good on the phone. And to be honest I had no idea what the fuck you were supposed to say to a grieving widow anyway. In the end, I decided to just bite the bullet, show up, and hope for the best.

The place Sims' wife had moved to was a run-down two-story apartment complex in serious need of a paint job. The front yard was little more than some patches of dead grass and brown shrubbery. The whole building and the grounds around it reeked of neglect. My first thought when I got there and saw the condition of the place was that Sims would have lost his damn mind from worry if he knew his wife was living in a shithole like this. I started trying to figure out what I could do to help her out as I made my way up the walk. I didn't know anything about survivor's benefits in the Corps, but I sure as hell thought there had to be something better for her than this.

At first, when the man answered her door, I thought I'd written the address down wrong. He was about my age, thin and cocky-looking, with a shitty little mustache. His clothes and hair smelled like weed. In confusion, I asked if this was where Tina Sims lived.

"Widow Sims!" he yelled back into the apartment, a laugh in his voice. "Someone's here to see you!"

When Tina came out, looking like she'd just gotten out of bed even though it was mid-afternoon, I recognized her instantly from Sims's photos. I told her who I was, and that I was a friend of her husband's.

"I ain't got a husband anymore," she sneered. "What I got now is a monthly check."

Tina Sims didn't want to talk to me, and wouldn't let me in the house. Not that I wanted to go in by that point, anyway. It was pretty clear she wasn't grieving Rob, and that she'd quickly found someone else to spend her time — and his death pension — with. If she hadn't been cheating on him the whole time he'd been gone, that is.

It ate at me, in the days and weeks afterwards. It killed me that Sims went to his death thinking his wife was faithful. Thinking that she loved him. That she missed him, and was waiting for him to come back home to her.

I don't know. Maybe it was better that he never found out the truth about her. But I fucking couldn't stand that he went to his grave being lied to like that. It still makes me sick to think about it.

I've always taken Sims and his wife as a cautionary tale. About what happens when you let your brain talk you into believing in shit that isn't real. Tina Sims lied to him, and shit all over him, and he never even knew it. And she'll never pay a price for betraying him. His marriage and his wife were the most important thing in his whole life, and it was all a goddamn lie. After that day, I could never quite look at any couple the same way again. I was always wondering who was fucking around on who. Who was lying to who.

I look down now at the woman sleeping peacefully beside me, and can't help but think that Sydney is about the furthest thing away from Tina Fucking Sims I can possibly imagine.

Don't go down that rabbit hole, motherfucker. This is just a mutual good time, nothing more.

But I'm not fooling myself. I haven't been able to stop thinking about wanting more with Sydney. Every time I leave her, I can hardly think about anything else but seeing her again. She's a fucking distraction. I should have put an end to this as soon as I realized she's not a woman I'm going to fuck a couple of times and then get sick of.

I lean back against the pillows and close my eyes, pissed at myself for even thinking about her like this. I am *not* in the market for an old lady. I should get up out of this bed, tell her goodbye, and go sink my dick into one of the club girls to get her out of my head. But I know I'm not about to do that.

There's not one of them that can hold a candle to her. Hell, there's not a woman I can think of that can hold a candle to Sydney Banner.

Fuck. I'm in deep.

23

SYDNEY

The next day, at work, I'm dead on my feet, and yet somehow positively *giddy*.

I don't know how much sleep Gavin got, but I'm pretty sure it's even less than the couple of hours I managed. He was still awake when I drifted off to sleep, and when he gently shook me awake at just before five a.m., he had already started some breakfast for us in my kitchen.

"I didn't know what time you needed to get up," he murmured as he slid into bed next to me, "but I figured it was early, so you could get to the shop."

We ate a quick breakfast of eggs and toast, and then he took off and told me he'd see me later on. I wandered around my house getting ready half in a daze, my mind still full of him and my body pleasantly sore from lovemaking.

Even now, I can feel him in the ache between my legs and the slight rawness of my face from his beard — souvenirs reminding me that we spend the night together. That he was in my bed. That we shared our stories in the dark.

A tiny pang of guilt rises up inside me, threatening to ruin my good mood, but I push it back down. I feel a little bad that the version I told Gavin why I left Atlantic City left out some pretty important details.

I'd told Gavin that Devon was one of my father's gambling associates, so it's not like I left him out of the story completely. What I didn't tell him was that Devon and I were together for almost a year before I skipped town.

Devon took me under his wing after he offered to bring me on as part of his team. At first, he kept our relationship completely platonic, never letting on that he had any sexual interest in me at all. I let my guard down, little by little coming to trust him as much as I'd ever trusted anyone besides my father. When we did get involved, he began confiding in me more regarding the "business" side of the house. I learned about some of his less than ethical dealings with some of the other members of the team. I also eventually learned, without his knowledge, that he was skimming money off the top of the organization before he paid us.

I was a high earner for Devon. I had a knack for being able to disguise myself and pass unnoticed. Once I had determined I wanted to leave Atlantic City and start somewhere fresh, I calculated that in the three years I'd worked for him he'd skimmed almost fifty-thousand dollars from me. It was money that I took back, the day I left, leaving him a note to that effect and telling him I was finished with Atlantic City and with the team.

I feel bad skipping over that part with Gavin. I know I should have told him about the texts I've received from Devon, and that there's a slight possibility that he might be serious about coming after me. I can't help but shake the feeling that Gavin would think I'd been lying to him if he knew, when that's not what I was doing at all — not intentionally, anyway. It's just that right then in the moment, things felt really *good*, laying here beside him. I didn't want to wreck the mood, and get him all riled up and saying things like *why the fuck didn't you tell me this before*, and *we have to immediately go buy fifteen security cameras for every angle of every room in your house*, and *I'm rearranging my life so I can spend twenty-four hours a day keeping an eye on you and making sure you're safe.*

Gavin would be angry if he knew I'd withheld all that from him. I know that. I try to tell my conscience not to feel so guilty about it. He is just trying to protect me, and I'd be lying if I said that doesn't make me feel sort of… well, not *loved*, exactly, but at least *valued*. But I also know he'd just worry *way* more than necessary. In my mind, there's a thin line between protection and ownership. *And Gavin doesn't own me*, I argue in my head, jutting out my chin defiantly. Being part of the team in Atlantic City was sort of like being owned. Our time was rarely our own, and everything we won had to be turned over to Devon first, before he would pay us our cut.

I don't want to be owned anymore. I've been taking care of myself practically my whole life. I'm used to going it alone. It's why I came to Tanner Springs. And I'm not going to feel guilty for keeping some of my secrets to myself.

Except, I kind of still do.

Just after the morning rush, the shop bell rings. I look up to see Gavin striding in. He flashes me a rare smile and I can't help but grin back at him.

"Hey there," he rumbles.

"Hey yourself," I answer, biting my lip at the memory of last night. "You don't have your to-go cup."

"Not here for a coffee today."

"Oh? What are you here for?" I smirk.

"You." He leans in close, his lips grazing my ear. "And you better stop biting that lip, or I'll have to take you in the back and bite it for you."

A little shiver of excitement runs down my spine.

"I think the customers would get a little suspicious," I reply huskily.

"Let 'em," he growls.

Is it getting warm in here, or is it just me?

I glance nervously around at the shop. Over at her customary table, Beverly is looking at us, a curious expression on her face.

"Uh," I stammer, clearing my throat. "Customers. Customers are looking at us."

He takes a step back and rolls his eyes. "Killjoy."

I can't help but laugh at that. "So, did you really just come to pay me a visit? You sure you aren't angling for a free muffin?"

"Well, I wouldn't turn it down," he says, eyes twinkling. "But I came to tell you I'm coming to pick you up later. On the bike."

"You came to *tell* me," I repeat pointedly. "Not *ask* me."

"Damn straight," he grins. "So be ready."

I roll my eyes. "You need a serious lesson in manners, you know that?"

He shrugs. "It's been tried. Didn't take."

With a wink, he turns and saunters out of the shop. I'm left standing there, grinning like an idiot out of a mixture of amusement and exasperation. I don't know how he manages not to be completely infuriating.

"Is that the man who came to install your fire extinguisher?"

I'm jolted out of my thoughts by Beverly, who has come up to the counter while I've been daydreaming.

"Oh! Uh, yes, that's him." I'm hoping my voice doesn't sound as shaky as I think it does.

She eyes me speculatively. "That's a very *capable*-looking handyman you've got there," she says, raising a thinly-penciled brow above her tortoise-shell frames.

I try an innocent laugh. "He's not actually a handyman. He just knew my old extinguisher didn't work, and got me a new one."

"He's a member of that motorcycle gang, isn't he? The Lords of Carnage?"

I can't quite read the look in Beverly's face, but I have to guess it's disapproval. "Yes," I say, trying not to sound defensive. "He's a regular customer here in the shop, if you can believe that."

"Hm." She nods, and stares at me evenly. "You know, the paper says that gang is behind all this recent crime in town," she observes. "Some of the letters to the editor do, anyway."

I draw back for a moment in genuine surprise. "I can't imagine that's true, Beverly," I say honestly. "No matter what the paper says. Not from what I've seen of Gavin, anyway. He's installed security cameras around here for me, all of his own accord. He seems more worried about the crimes than I do."

"I see." She looks up and around, and notices the camera Brick has installed above the front door. "That was very nice of him, wasn't it?"

"Yes," I admit. "It was. Though at the time, I wasn't very gracious about it."

"Am I correct in assuming there's something going on between the two of you?" she asks with a curious gleam in her eye.

I open my mouth to deny it, but instead I hesitate. Because for some reason, I kind of *want* to tell someone about Gavin and me. Even though I have no idea what we're really doing together, I can't help but wish I could talk about it like we're a normal couple.

The realization that I actually *want* this to be a *relationship*, or something, hits me like a bolt from the blue.

Shit. This isn't good.

"I, uh… That is, yes, there is something going on between us. It's nothing serious," I add quickly.

"Are you sure?" She gives me a slight smile. "Because from the way he looks at you, I'm not entirely convinced."

"I think he's just…" *Horny? Down to fuck?* "A little possessive."

"Well. As long as he treats you well. He is quite attractive, isn't he, even with all the tattoos?"

My mind flashes to last night, and the ripple of his muscles as he stroked his hard length. My face flushes hot. "Yes, he certainly is," I agree.

"You may be right about what's being said in the paper," she says, nodding thoughtfully. "It's always been sort of a rag, after all. I wouldn't be surprised if they're barking up the wrong tree. All the same, though, Sydney, you will be careful, won't you?"

"Don't worry," I assure her. "I'm probably safer with Gavin around than I've ever been."

While we've been talking, the door to the shop opens again. It's kolache guy. I instinctively glance over to the table where he usually meets his friends, but they haven't come in yet this morning. Instead, as I watch in surprise, he sets a small hardcover book and his glasses case down on Beverly's table. She gives him a quick wave as he comes up to the counter.

"I hope you're not out of kolaches yet," he greets me in a jovial tone. "Beverly," he murmurs, turning to her.

"Hello, Bradley," she smiles back at him. The two of them look at me expectantly. I'm momentarily discombobulated, and I'm not sure if it's from learning that Kolache Guy actually has a name, or that the two of them seem to be on some sort of... *date?*

"Oh! Kolaches. I've made the poppyseed ones today," I say hastily, and move toward the case. "You'll have to tell me what you think."

"I'm sure they'll be delicious," Beverly assures me. "We'll take two. And I'd like a refill on my latte."

"A plain coffee for me," Bradley adds. "And I'll take the bill."

Beverly smiles demurely, thanks him, and moves off to their table. I ring them up and tell him the total — and almost fall over in surprise when he puts the quarter he gets back in change in the tip jar.

"Well, son of a bitch," I murmur to myself as he goes to join Beverly.

The rest of the day passes without anything as surprising as Beverly and Bradley's book reading date. Business is brisk, but not enough to keep my mind from wandering to unbidden thoughts of last night and Gavin. By the time Hailey shows up for her shift, I've probably looked at the clock three dozen times.

"How did closing go last night?" I ask her.

"Good," she informs me. "Except that there was a big rush at the end of the night. I didn't get out of here until almost ten."

I frown. "That's not good. At least it wasn't a school night." Today's Saturday, though, and if last night was any indication, she might get slammed again tonight.

"It wasn't that big of a deal," Hailey says amiably. "More hours equals more money."

"True. But I don't love the idea of you being here alone so late." I think all Gavin's paranoid warnings about safety and security are getting to me. Maybe it's time for me to get serious about hiring some more help.

Hailey and I go over some details, and I'm reminding her she can always call me if she has any problems when I get a text from him.

Got held up a little. Be there in an hour or so.

I frown. I'd rather not wait around here for another hour. And besides, I realize the delay would give me time to take a shower if I run home.

Can you pick me up at my place instead?

You trying to seduce me?

I laugh.

I promise I won't even let you in the house. I'm waiting for that ride on your motorcycle.

My heart speeds up as I read his final text:

See you soon babe

I shove my phone back into my pocket, feeling happy and excited. After saying a quick goodbye to Hailey, I slip out the back and drive home to get ready.

24

BRICK

The address that Oz gives Rock to meet up with him and some of the other Death Devils turns out to be a run-down bar at the northwestern edge of their territory.

It's early afternoon on a hot, dusty day, and we look to be the only customers here. I'm not sure whether that's by design or not, but when we show up, a grizzled-looking bartender wordlessly shows us to a back room, where Oz and his men are already waiting.

Just like we agreed on in church, Rock has brought Angel, Ghost, and me with him. In a sign of good faith to Oz, we don't bring any backup for security.

Oz has two of his men posted at the entrance to the room for security. One of them is about my size. The other one is almost as big as our brother Beast, who's six foot seven and built like a brick shit house. The big one motions to a table just inside the door and tells us to leave our pieces there. Rock looks at us and nods. Reluctantly, I pull my Glock out of the waistband of my jeans and set it on the table with the others.

Oz is sitting silently at a wide table in the center of the room. Two men are flanking him. We approach and Rock offers his hand. The two men shake, and we sit.

"I've looked further into the situation with the Iron Spiders," Oz begins without preamble. "My connections tell me they have formed a business partnership with a club to your north. The Outlaw Sons."

"What kind of partnership?" Rock grunts.

"Shipments between them. What kind of product they're moving is unclear," Oz replies, lifting a hand to stroke a long, dark beard flecked with gray. "What they do know is that your territory lies directly between theirs. So any shipments that pass between them currently would have to be routed around Lords of Carnage territory, to the east or west."

"There's no easy path going west," I remark. "Better roads to the east."

"Yes," Oz agrees glancing at me. "Which would put them through Death Devils territory."

"If it were me," Angel speaks up, "I'd be inclined to take the long view. That the shortest distance between two points is a straight line."

Oz nods once. "As would I."

We sit in silence for a moment, contemplating this. Suddenly, it's starting to look pretty likely that all the shit going down in Tanner Springs is an attempt to take down our club by fucking with our town and hoping the crimes will get pinned on us.

"Goddamn cowards," Angel seethes. "They wanna take us on, why don't they grow some fucking balls and do it face to face?"

"This calls for all out war," Ghost rasps, looking at Rock. "The Spiders almost killed Hawk's old lady, and now this. They're not going to stop until either their club or ours is destroyed. It's time to cut off the head to kill the body. Black has to die."

The rest of us nod. There's no way we can let this stand. The Spiders' president will have to pay for this with his life. It's the only way to stop this for good.

"Oz. It looks like we have a common interest in protecting both our territories," Rock says, his jaw tensing. "What can we expect from your club?"

For a moment, Oz is perfectly still. Then he forms his hands into a steeple.

"It is true, neither of us benefits from seeing the Iron Spiders get stronger," he says. "We will protect our territory at all costs. And protecting our territory includes maintaining close ties with the Lords of Carnage." He meets Rock's eyes.

"You will have men when you need them. As long as our goals remain the same."

Oz pushes back his chair. His men stand in unison.

"Gentlemen," he says.

The four of us get to our feet.

"I'll be in touch, Oz," Rock grunts.

We turn and recover our guns, then walk out of the deserted bar back to our bikes.

No one talks as we start up our engines and head back toward Tanner Springs. We're all thinking about the same thing.

As of now, there's no going back. There will be no rest for the Lords or Carnage until the Spiders are done.

It's us or them. The choice is clear.

When we reach the clubhouse, Rock calls an emergency meeting. He tells all the brothers what we've learned. Everyone is in grim agreement about what needs to be done.

Rock tells Tweak to use his tech skills and contacts to locate the Iron Spiders clubhouse. Like many MCs, their club location is a closely guarded secret. But Tweak has never let us down before. Once he's figured out where their spider nest is, we'll send some of our men out there to surveil and place cameras so we can see their comings and goings. Especially to see if there are any patterns to Black's movements.

And when he's likely to be alone, and vulnerable.

At the end of church, Rock bangs the gavel, and we all file out in silence. Some of the men go home to their families, to prepare their old ladies. We'll figure out our strategy in the upcoming days. Right now, it's the calm before the storm.

As for me, I can only think of one thing.

Seeing Sydney.

*   *   *

When I texted Sydney before we went into church, she asked me to meet her at her place instead of the coffee shop since I was going to be late. When I get to her address, she fairly flies out of her front door before I've even had a chance to park the bike.

"See!" she says with a grin, running up to me. "I locked the door behind me. I promised you I wouldn't let you in."

There's something about the way she looks at me -- eyes shining, her hair streaming loose behind her -- that makes me feel so damn happy that before I know it, my throat constricts. I have to stop myself from talking for a second until I can get hold of myself.

"You're looking damn good, babe," I finally manage to choke out, hoping she doesn't notice the gruffness in my voice.

"I had good incentive," she murmurs as I pull her into my arms. I kiss her, deeply, and when she draws away she gives me a dazzling smile that almost makes me choke up again.

"So," I say, clearing my throat and releasing her. "You ever been on one of these things?"

"Nope." She shrugs. "About damn time I do, though, don't you think?"

"I do," I nod. I straddle the bike and nod behind me. "Get on and get comfortable. Feet on the pegs. Arms around me."

She does as she's told, wrapping her arms tight around my waist and leaning into me. It feels good. Damn good.

"Where are we going?" she asks.

"You'll see," I tell her. The question sobers me, but I start the engine and pull away from the curb.

I need to talk to Sydney about some things, and what I need to say is probably better said once I've introduced her to some people. This isn't the way I was hoping things would go today, but I don't have a choice.

Riding back to Tanner Springs after meeting with Oz, I had some time to think about what's going on between Sydney and me. As much as I've tried to resist it — resist her — she's gotten inside my head. Inside my skin. She's mouthy, and prickly, and feisty as hell. She's as stubborn as they come, and she's fucking beautiful, and unlike any other woman I've ever met in my life.

As we ride through the streets and I steer us toward our destination, I realize I'm weirdly nervous. It's not a feeling I'm used to. Then it dawns on me what it is.

Hope.

I'm actually hoping for a future. With Sydney.

It's so fucking ridiculous I start to laugh. It takes a goddamn club war and the possible end to the Lords for me to believe in anything other than the actual moment I'm living in.

I'm heading into something that I might not survive. I've done that plenty of times in my life. I've never been scared of death.

Except this time it's different. This time, there's something on the other side that I'd do anything to keep. Someone on the other side I'd do anything to protect.

For the first time, I think I might understand how Ghost feels when he looks at Jenna and his kids. Or Hawk when he looks at Sam.

Behind me, Sydney snuggles closer. I can feel the steady rise and fall of her breathing.

It's time for her to know more about my life than just that I wear a leather cut. It's time for her to understand what it means to be a Lord of Carnage. For her to understand what this life means. At least enough to decide whether she wants to stick around, or whether she wants me to leave her the fuck alone. I don't know everything about her life, but I know she's gone through a lot to get where she is. I don't want to fuck that up for her.

To be honest, I'm scared she'll walk away.

Hell, that might be the best thing for both of us.

If she does, I tell myself I'll be fine.

But I think I might be full of shit.

25
SYDNEY

We pull up to a nondescript two-story building with a flat roof and a large gravel parking lot in the front. At first, I have no idea where Gavin has brought me, but when I see the row of motorcycles parked off to one side, something clicks.

"Is this where your club meets?" I ask him after he's cut the bike.

"Yeah. This is the clubhouse," he rumbles.

It's not marked in any way, which I suppose is on purpose. Gavin waits as I climb down from the seat, then stands up himself.

"I figured it was time you meet some of my people," he says, and catches my hand in his. We walk up to the front door, holding hands, and I'm not sure what to make of any of this. We've never had any sort of conversation about what's been happening between us. And now, he's holding my hands and taking me to meet his friends.

I raise my other hand and rake it self-consciously through my wind-blown hair. I wish I'd known I was about to be presented to what amounts to Gavin's family. I don't have a lot of time to let my nerves get the better of me, though, because we're already through the door and striding through a large, open bar area. A dozen or more men are there, all of them large, tattooed, and dangerous looking. A handful of women are there, too. More than a few of the crowd stop what they're doing to look at us as we come in. Over behind the bar itself, a tall, busty blond widens her eyes in obvious surprise.

One of the men detaches himself from a group and comes over to us, an easy, panty-melting grin on his face. He's drop-dead gorgeous, with short-cropped hair and looks that could easily land him on the cover of a men's magazine.

"Well, well! What have we here, brother?" he says, slapping Gavin on the back. "This *is* a first! Hello, little lady." He turns his megawatt smile on me. "I'm Gunner. Brick's closest friend and fellow Marine. I don't believe I've had the pleasure."

I smile at him, suddenly shy but trying not to show it. "Hi. I'm Sydney."

"A beautiful name for a beautiful lady," he nods, and winks at me. "How the hell did you end up with an ugly fucker like him?"

"Gunner," Brick mutters in a warning tone.

"Lighten up, brother. You know you love me." Gunner chuckles at the storm clouds gathering on Gavin's face. "Hey, y'all, this is Sydney," Gunner calls to the room. "For some reason, she's decided to give Brick the time of day."

"I'm really fucking beginning to regret this," Gavin mutters beside me.

Gunner's general announcement seems to have broken some sort of spell, because a few more people start to come up to us. A strikingly pretty brunette with long, glossy hair approaches, a welcoming smile on her face.

"Hi, there!" she says, holding out her hand. "I'm Sam. It's really nice to meet you."

"It's nice to meet you, too," I say, shaking with her.

"I'm with Hawk," she continues, nodding her head toward a muscular, tanned, heavily tattooed man who comes up behind her

"Hi," I say to the man. He nods once and slips his arm around Sam's waist.

"Is this your first time at the clubhouse?" Sam asks. "I'm gathering yes."

"Yeah. Honestly, I didn't even know we were coming here," I admit, looking up at Brick and giving him a teasing frown. He shrugs and clasps my hand a little tighter.

Sam laughs. "Trial by fire, huh, Brick?" she chides him. "Well, the men aren't as tough as they let on, no matter what they like to think."

"Is that right?" Hawk rumbles down at her.

"Present company excluded, of course," Sam smirks, leaning up to give him a peck on the cheek.

"Hi, I'm Jenna," another woman's voice says. I turn to see a petite blonde with gorgeous blue eyes. "Haven't I seen you coming out of that new coffee shop in town? Do you work there?"

"Actually, I'm the owner," I tell her. "That's how Ga… Brick and I met. He used to come in for coffee a couple times a week."

"Oh, shit!" Gunner snorts. "You're the muffin lady! Damn, you seduced him with tasty baked goods!"

A few of the other men gathered around us start laughing uproariously. Gavin looks a little pissed, but seems to take it in stride.

"Okay, okay, you fuckers," he mutters. "I defy you to resist Sydney's blueberry muffins, though. It takes a real man to admit when he's beat by a pastry."

"Hey, Sydney," Sam says, "Can I get you a beer or something?"

"Beer would be great," I smile.

"Jewel!" Sam calls toward the attractive bartender. "This is Sydney! Our girl needs a beer!"

And, just like that, it seems I'm accepted. A cold bottle is handed to me a minute later, and before I know it, I'm caught up in an ever-shifting conversation with all sorts of people who want to ask me questions or tell me embarrassing stories about the man they know as Brick. It's...

Fun.

Like, *really* fun. I essentially haven't done anything except for work and go home to sleep since I got to Tanner Springs. I never bothered to try to make friends — force of habit from my old life, I guess. I didn't even know I was missing anything, until now.

But here? Laughing and joking with these people I don't even know — people that most law-abiding citizens would consider scary and dangerous — I feel at home, and *safe* in a way I don't ever remember feeling. Back in Atlantic City, I knew a lot of people, but in the circles I ran in, you knew better than to trust anyone but yourself. Here, with Gavin holding my hand like it's the most natural thing in the world, somehow I feel completely at ease with total strangers who accept me just because I'm with him.

Somehow, Jenna and Sam and I end up over at the bar with Jewel the bartender, talking and laughing over our beers. Jenna and Sam tell me the stories of how they met their men. Apparently, Jenna, who's married to Ghost, the Sergeant at Arms, had a fling with him a few years back, and then left town for a while. When she came back to Tanner Springs, they reconnected, and they've been together ever since. They have two little kids, a boy and a girl. From time to time, she glances over at Ghost adoringly as she tells their story. Listening to Jenna talk about her family, it's incredibly clear from the look on her face how happy she is.

Sam tells me that she and Hawk have been together less than a year. Funnily enough, they met at Jenna and Ghost's wedding. Sam's a photographer, and Jenna hired her to take pictures of the day.

"Holy hell, did the two of us spar when we first met," Sam's shaking her head. "He was, and still is, a total pain in the ass sometimes. But even though I never would have believed it in a million years, he's the sweetest, most loving man I ever met."

I glance over at the glowering, tattooed man, who's over by the pool tables talking to Brick and Gunner. "Wow. Talk about not judging a book by its cover," I chuckle. The other two women laugh.

Just as I'm about to look away at the three men, Gavin glances up toward me. Our eyes lock, and a wave of heat courses through my body.

"Looks like Brick is laying a claim to you," Jenna remarks. I drag my gaze away from him and look at her.

"What do you mean, laying a claim?" I ask, my pulse speeding up just a notch.

"Well…" Jenna says, sliding her eyes toward Sam, and then back to me. "I've known Brick for a while now, and I sure as hell have never seen him show more than a passing interest in any woman. He sure as *hell* has never brought one here."

From the other side of the bar, Jewel nods. "The Lords take this club, and this clubhouse, pretty damn seriously," she tells me. "This club is a family, Sydney. If you're here with him, it means something."

Holy hell. My brain starts to feel like it's spinning in my head. I think back to my conversation with Beverly earlier today in the shop, when I told her what was happening between Gavin and me was nothing serious. The words she said in reply ring in my head.

"Are you sure? Because from the way he looks at you, I'm not entirely convinced."

"Ready to go?"

I startle out of my thoughts to see that Gavin has appeared at my side.

"So soon?" I ask, a little regretfully.

"I want to show you someplace else," he murmurs into my hair. "And then we need to talk."

I turn back to the women, and can't help take note of their expressions as they look at the two of us. Jewel's face is full of amused excitement. Samantha is grinning conspiratorially at me. Jenna... well, her face registers something beyond just happiness for a new couple. As she looks between us, there's a note of tension that appears on her face. Almost as though she knows what Gavin wants to talk to me about.

"You two have a good night," she says to both of us, reaching out to give my hand a warm squeeze. "It was really great to meet you, Sydney."

"It was wonderful to meet you all, too," I say sincerely. Brick puts his hand on the small of my back and guides me back outside to his motorcycle.

"So, where are you taking me?" I ask him teasingly as he puts a leg over his bike and motions for me to get on.

"It's a surprise," he growls, starting up the bike.

"Everything about you is a surprise, Brick Malone," I murmur into his ear, wrapping my arms around him.

It's true. Gavin has been nothing but surprises since the day we met.

And the biggest one of all? I'm starting to think I like it.

26
BRICK

I've never brought any woman to the clubhouse before bringing Sydney there tonight. But bringing her out to my lake place is even crazier.

Except for Gunner the few times he's been out here fishing with me, and the occasional guys delivering shit from the local home improvement store, no one but me has ever stepped inside my house. I sure as hell have never had a woman in my bed. This place is my sanctuary. The whole reason I bought it in the first place was to be alone.

But for some reason, I want Sydney here tonight. Because what I have to tell her is important. And hell, Sydney is important. Somehow, without my even realizing it, she's gotten under my skin. She's broken through my defenses.

If I want any kind of future with her to happen, I have to tell her what she might be in for. And I want to do that in a place where it's no one else but just the two of us. I'll take her back to her place in a heartbeat if she tells me that's what she wants. But first, I want to push the rest of the world aside. Just for a few hours. Just to have her with me, all to myself, no matter what happens afterwards.

I feel rather than hear Sydney draw in a breath as I round the corner of the gravel drive and my house first comes into view. The house itself still isn't much to look at from the outside — I'll get around to painting and shit once the interior's done. But the view of the lake behind it is spectacular. The water is crystalline, with the early evening sun glancing off the surface. Across the lake to the west, a bank of thick clouds is slowly rolling this way, promising a storm later on this evening, but for right now the lake is calm.

"This is where you live?" Sydney breathes as I take her hand and lead her to the front porch.

"Yeah," I grunt. "Not much from the outside. But I'm working on it."

"My God, Gavin. It's so beautiful." Her eyes are shining with admiration as she stares toward the lake. "You must love it here."

I don't say anything as I let her inside. It never occurred to me to think about this place in those terms. The solitude here suits me, it's true. And she's right, the lake looks straight out of a postcard. Watching her take it all in, I feel a new appreciation for it all.

If she was here with you, you would love it here.

The thought comes unbidden. I sit with it for a second, then push it away.

"Do you want something to drink?" I ask her gruffly. Now that we're inside — now that she's in my space — I'm starting to feel kind of awkward. The main living area is stripped down to the bare walls and subflooring. The only furniture in the living room is my old leather couch, a flat-screen TV, and a king-sized mattress over by the fireplace. It's hardly comfortable enough for a guest. I didn't really think of that when I decided to bring her out here.

"No, I'm fine," she says, turning to me with wide eyes. "Are you doing all the work yourself?"

"Pretty much," I shrug.

"This place is going to be amazing when you're done with it." I can see she means it. Her words make me hope that she'll be around to see the house when I *do* finish it.

There's that word again. Hope.

I grab a beer for myself and take her out to the back deck, which is the one part of the house that's completely finished. I even have decent furniture out there, because it's where I spend so much of my time when I'm here. We sit down on the long, low sectional that faces the lake. I resist the urge to take her into my arms. I want to see her face for this conversation.

"Did you buy this place because it reminded you of Seneca Lake, where you grew up?" she asks as she settles in.

For a moment, I'm floored. It's on the tip of my tongue to say no, because I didn't. Not consciously, anyway. But now that she's said it, I realize that this little lake, with its homes set back far enough that it almost looks uninhabited, *does* kind of remind me of Seneca. It has the same calm, peaceful feeling — or rather, the peacefulness I always *wanted* to feel there growing up, but didn't because I never seemed able to escape the hell of my life at home.

"Maybe," is all I can say, as I wonder how Sydney managed to figure out something about me that I didn't even know myself.

"I really enjoyed meeting your friends, Gavin," Sydney murmurs. "They're… different than I expected."

"Different how?"

"I don't know." She thinks for a moment. "I guess I thought they'd be not so… *nice.*"

Laughter rumbles out of me. "I don't think I've ever heard Hawk or Ghost called nice."

A smile flits across her face, but then she grows serious. "I mean it." She shrugs, and looks down at her hands. "At least they were to me. Most of the people I've known in my life *haven't* been."

"The club's a family, Sydney. You were there with me. So, they consider you one of them. One of us."

Her eyes meet mine. "Am I?" she asks.

Holy shit. My heart starts pounding like a fucking jackhammer.

"Sydney," I say. My voice drops about an octave, because I'm trying to keep it steady. "That's what I wanted to talk to you about."

I'm just trying to keep emotion out of this, and tell her what she needs to know. But for some reason, she misinterprets my words. "Oh. No, look, Gavin," she half-laughs. "I'm not trying to ask for anything. I mean, I get it. We barely know each other. And hell, we've barely even ever had a conversation, other than after sex sometimes." She starts waving a hand between us, like she's physically trying to clear the air. "It's fine. No reason for us to pretend this is more —."

"Sydney," I bark, grabbing her hand in mid-air. She stops abruptly and stares at me in surprise. "Will you please shut the hell up for a second?"

She gives me a dark look and tries to pull her hand away. "Well, there's no need to be rude."

"Are you going to stop putting words in my mouth and listen to me?"

"Jesus," she complains, and tries to pull away again. This time I let her. "Fine," she says, crossing her arms. "Talk."

"Fuck," I mutter. "This isn't going the way I wanted it to."

The fact is, I don't know exactly how I expected it to go. I didn't plan this out very well. In my mind, I skipped over the part where I told her all the stuff I needed to, and went straight to the part where I took her inside and fucked her until we both passed out.

Sydney is still sitting there, her arms crossed and her eyes stubbornly fixed on a spot on the ground about five feet in front of her. I heave a deep sigh and try again.

"Look," I say. "First. I brought you to the clubhouse for a reason." I reach up and cup her chin, lifting it toward me until her eyes reluctantly meet mine. "I wanted you to meet my brothers — my family — for a reason."

"What's the reason?" she half-whispers.

I don't know how to put it into words, but the only thing I can do is open my damn mouth and hope for the best.

"I… wanted to give you a chance to see what you'd be getting into. To back out if you want."

"Oh, for God's sake. Back out of what?" Sydney cries, rolling her eyes in exasperation. "Gavin, what the hell are you talking about?"

"Sydney." I rake a hand roughly through my hair. "There's some shit going down with the club right now. It's not the safest place to be. I know you came to Tanner Springs to get away from Atlantic City. To have a calmer, simpler life someplace new." I snort and shake my head. "But if calm and simple is what you want, then I'm afraid getting mixed up with me is about the last fucking thing you want to do."

"So… the club's in danger?" she asks.

"Not exactly. But the club is about to enter into a war, and shit is bound to escalate pretty fast." I take her hand, which has fallen into her lap, and run the pad of my thumb over her palm. "I don't want you to get hurt. But more than anything, I want you to know that being around me might not be the safest place going forward."

Sydney seems lost in thought. "Does this have anything to do with the break-ins and stuff in Tanner Springs?"

"Yes."

"And you're trying to protect me, when it sounds like you're actually the one in danger?"

"I guess. Yes."

"Thank you," she says quietly.

I take that to mean she's done. My stomach lurches, but I ignore it.

"So. I can take you back to your place, if you want."

"What?" She's confused.

"If you want to go back," I offer with a sinking heart. "I can take you."

For a moment her face goes totally blank.

Then she *laughs.*

"Goddamnit, Gavin!" she cries, rolling her eyes. "What the hell is wrong with you, anyway?"

"What?" I am *not* used to women talking like this to me. Or anyone, for that matter. Anger starts rising up in me, but I try to tamp it down.

"What's wrong with *me*?" I bark back. "For trying to protect you, and telling you that being associated with me is a bad idea?" *Fuck.* I should never have told her any of this. I should have just stopped coming around her. Let her think I'd lost interest. That would have been the safest thing to do.

Regret, so deep and slicing it's almost physically painful, hits me. I set out trying to protect this crazy girl. And now it turns out I may have done the exact opposite.

"Gavin," she begins, with a patience I can tell is forced. "Thank you for thinking of me. I appreciate it. But I can make my own choices, despite what you might think. I'm no shrinking violet." Her face softens, and she lets out a low chuckle. "Did I ever tell you that Violet is my first name? I go by my middle name because my dad never liked it. 'You're not going to be a shrinking violet,' he used to say to me." She trains her eyes on me. "And I'm not. So don't treat me like one."

"Is it treating you like a shrinking violet to tell you hanging around me might put you in danger?" I challenge.

"No," she says gently. "That's treating me like an equal. And so is letting me make my own choices." She meets my gaze. "Do you want me around? Ignoring any danger, and anything else going on? Do you want *this*?"

Fuck. This girl. How did I get roped into a conversation about *feelings*?

"Yeah," I say gruffly. "I do."

"I do too." She takes a deep breath and lets it out. "So maybe let's just go from there. Okay?"

I turn away for a second, and look out over the lake. When she says it like that, it sounds simple. Obvious, even. *Shit*. Is this how it happens? Is this how you get sucked down the rabbit hole, and end up laying your heart and your soul on the line for someone who could betray you in a heartbeat?

Then I look back at Sydney, who's still sitting there waiting. And I remember how she looked sitting at the bar, laughing with Sam and Jenna and Jewel. How natural she looked there. Like one of the old ladies.

Like *my* old lady.

Enough talk.

27
SYDNEY

"Come here," he commands. We're back inside now, standing next to the large mattress that's on the floor in the main living room.

I do exactly as he says, of course. Without hesitation. As much as I push back on his caveman act, in the bedroom, he's the boss. That much is clear.

And I realize now I wouldn't have it any other way.

Heat pools between my legs as he pulls me into his arms. But instead of immediately bringing his mouth down on mine, he lifts my chin with his finger until our eyes are locked on each other and we're only inches apart.

"I'm going to fuck you until you're screaming my name, baby. You're gonna do everything I say, and you're gonna love every second of it. And then you're going to come all over my cock."

"Yes," I say breathlessly. I'm already wet, so wet I can feel my juices beginning to coat my upper thighs. There's a look on his face that's so full of naked lust it's almost *angry*. And oh God, it's turning me on. Every time we've had sex has been so good it's hard to believe it's even real. But there's something about the animal way his eyes are devouring me now. A little shiver runs up my spine as I wonder what he's going to do to me. How he's going to use me.

God, I want him to use every inch of me.

"On your knees," he growls. He yanks off his shirt and unbuttons his jeans, pushing them down until his hard, proud length springs free. I get on my knees on the mattress, my mouth exactly level with his cock. A bead of precum is already forming at the tip, and I'm actually craving his taste, craving the way his cock will feel as I try to take as much of him in as I can.

Gavin fists a hand in my hair and guides my head toward him. I look up into his eyes, biting my lip in anticipation. His eyes are hooded, his face dark with stormy need.

I've never seen him so hard, so large. His length is pulsing in front of me. I raise a hand and circle his shaft with my fingers, then lean forward slightly and run my tongue over his head. Above me, Gavin gasps and stops breathing for a moment. The skin is hot, and tight. I slide my lips over the tip of him, tasting his saltiness, and swirl my tongue around him again. His fist tightens slightly in my hair. I know what I'm doing to him, I *love* what I'm doing to him. More than anything right now, I want to make him come like this, want to make him lose control, and know that *I* did that, that I'm the one who makes him like this.

I moan low in my throat as I take him in deeper. Slowly, I pull back, and then push forward again, until he's hitting the back of my throat. "Fuck," he rasps. "Sydney. *Fuck*. Feel what you do to me." A thrill skates across my skin hearing his words. I begin to slowly bob, paying attention to every breath, every gasp, every pulse. Between my legs I'm throbbing with need, but he tastes so good that this is all I care about. Brick begins to thrust, ever so slightly, in time with my mouth. His taste grows saltier as he leaks more precum. I know he's close. I'm hoping against hope he'll let me...

"Jesus," he growls, pulling away from me suddenly. "That's too goddamn good, Sydney. But I want more. So much more."

He steps back, his cock glistening in the fading light. Behind him, through the floor to ceiling windows, I see the storm clouds that were across the lake are growing closer. The sky is blackening behind him as he stands majestically above me, all hard muscles and tense, barely controlled lust.

"Take off your clothes and stand in front of me."

My entire body thrumming, I do as he says, until I'm standing before him. There are windows open, and the temperature is already dropping with the upcoming storm. My skin cools and my nipples harden. Between my legs, the slick wetness chills in the air.

Gavin is slowly stroking himself as his eyes rake across my naked body. "Fucking Christ, Sydney," he rasps. "I can't wait to sink myself inside you."

"Do it, Gavin," I breathe, my voice sliding into a whine. "Please, I need it so much."

"Not yet, babe. Not yet." He moves forward and lies down on the bed. "Straddle my face," he orders me.

My face flushes hot. I hesitate for a moment, but he's not taking no for an answer.

"Straddle me, Sydney. I want you to come on my tongue."

My throbbing pussy makes the decision for me. I kneel down and do as he says, shuddering as his hot breath teases the sensitive, quivering skin on my thighs.

"Fuck my tongue, baby. Take your pleasure."

He grabs my hips and slides me toward him, until his tongue slides hot and wet against my clit. I cry out, bucking involuntarily because it's already so good. My body takes over, and soon I'm nothing but need, thrusting slowly against his tongue, reaching up to pinch my own nipples as I feel like I might just lose my mind before this is over. Brick groans deeply, the vibrations teasing my pussy, and I know he's stroking himself. I hear my voice, far away, as I say incoherent things, climbing higher and higher so fast it's dizzying. Then Gavin grabs my hands in his to steady me, and I hang on tight as my body freezes, then convulses as my orgasm tears through me. I hear myself calling his name, over and over, as my whole body quakes. He continues to lap at me until finally, finally, I can't take anymore and collapse to the side.

There's movement, and then he's on top of me, his salty lips devouring mine.

"You taste so fucking good, do you know that?" he growls against my skin. "Taste yourself, baby. I could lick you and eat you forever. Jesus, you're delicious."

I'm exhausted, so spent I'm not sure I can even sit up, but there's still something missing, an ache I need to have satisfied.

"Please, Gavin, I want to feel you. I want you inside —."

"Look at me, baby." I open my eyes to see him towering above me. The storm clouds are gathered behind his head. As he pulls my hips roughly toward him, a brilliant flash of lightning splits the sky, followed by a loud crack of thunder. Gavin moves between my thighs. He drags his cock against my sensitive clit, finding my entrance as I gasp and angle towards him.

"You're mine," he growls. "Say it."

He thrusts roughly inside me. I cry out.

"Yes," I gasp. "I'm yours. Oh, God, yes."

He pulls out and thrusts again, even deeper. "Fuck!"

This. This is what I need. "Harder," I whisper. I want him to fill me. I want him to fuck me so hard I can feel it for days.

His eyes lock on mine, so intense I should be scared. I'm not. I want this. I want all of it.

He *slams* inside me. I cry out. He slams again. I can feel the climax begin to build, already. My body begins to shake. Every thrust takes me higher, I'm calling out to him, begging him for release. Then I feel it: my channel clenches around him, and a tsunami hits me from the inside out, waves of pleasure that make my entire body feel like it's liquid. In the midst of it all, I feel Gavin expand inside me, then explode in a burst of heat as he shouts my name.

I feel him wrap his arms around me with a gentleness that comes as a surprise after the intensity of our coupling. He pulls me against him as the storm begins, rain and wind battering against the windows. Drops come in through the screens and spatter the floor, but we just lie there, his massive body holding me, heating me with his warmth.

He doesn't speak. Neither do I. I can't. The intensity of the last few minutes has left me without words.

You're mine. Say it.

I've never thought of myself as wanting to belong to anyone. No one but myself.

But right now, the *only* thing I want is to be his.

28
BRICK

Sydney falls into a deep, exhausted sleep, snoring softly in my arms. I lie there and listen to the wind and rain.

When the storm ends, I go out onto the deck and watch the moon come out over the lake. The frogs are out, and their rhythmic song wafts toward me in the otherwise quiet night.

What just happened between Sydney and me... I'm not sure how to handle it.

I didn't mean to claim her. I didn't mean to demand that she tell me she's mine.

She did it, though. Without hesitation.

My dick hardens at the memory. I've never wanted a woman more than I want Sydney. Even now, not even an hour after I came so hard inside her I fucking saw stars, my balls are already starting to ache at the thought of having her again. Usually when I fuck a woman, having her once is enough to take away the mystery and put her out of my mind. But with Sydney, it's the exact opposite. Now that I know exactly how sweet she tastes... how wet for me she gets... the noises she makes just before she comes... the way her pussy clenches around me as she flies over the edge... I just want more. And more. I can't imagine ever getting enough of her.

I claimed her. She told me she's mine.

I want to fuck her until I know her body better than she knows it herself. I want her body to forget everything but my touch. Forget every other man who's ever touched her.

I want to take her to my bed every damn night. And wake up with her in it every morning. I want her to know she belongs to me. And I want everyone else to know it, too.

My mind drifts back to being with her earlier tonight at the clubhouse. Seeing her there with Jenna and Sam. How natural it looked. How fucking proud I was to look over and see her there. Gunner and some of the other brothers were giving me shit about her, and asking all sorts of questions about who she was and how the fuck she'd managed to corral me. It didn't really bother me, even though I pretended it did.

Now, thinking back on it, though, I'm feeling more than just pride. I'm realizing how far out of hand this whole thing has gotten with Sydney, without me even realizing it. Hell, how did I get from just going into a shop for a damn cup of coffee, to this, so quickly? I didn't even see it coming. All I did was go back to the Golden Cup a second time, and then before I knew it I was putting up security cameras for her, and fucking her in her back office, and now bringing her to a house I specifically bought so I could be alone. Taking her to my bed.

Shit.

Maybe taking her to the clubhouse tonight… maybe that was a mistake after all. I don't know what I was thinking. I've been too blind to see how far I've fallen for Sydney already. I don't need this kind of complication in my life.

Then why the fuck did you just claim her?

It was stupid. Logically, it was fucking stupid.

She doesn't know what it means to claim her. She doesn't know how serious it is for a man in an MC to say that to a woman.

Hell, she might not even have meant it when she said she was mine. She might not even remember it happened tomorrow.

But that's irrelevant. *I* know I asked it. Fuck, I *demanded* it.

And the heat of passion might have had something to do with it, but it's still true.

I want her. I fucking *want* her. I'm in love with her, I think.

I glance toward the window, into the house. I can just make out Sydney's sleeping form on the other side. My chest tightens as a wave of fierce protectiveness hits me, so strong it almost feels like a physical force.

It's never been like this with anyone. Not even close. I never even saw it coming.

Maybe it's just my dick doing my thinking for me. I try out the thought, but a snort of laughter rips out of me almost immediately. That's not what it is, and I know it. My dick knows it can get pussy wherever and whenever it wants. As goddamn amazing as the sex is with Sydney, I know it's more than that. A hell of a lot more. I've been drawn to her since the very beginning. Only I was a fucking idiot and never let myself see it until now. I didn't go into that fucking coffee shop the second time because my new coffee maker was still in the box. Or the third time. Hell, the goddamn thing is *still* sitting in my kitchen right now, unopened, not thirty feet away from where Sydney is.

I went because of her. Because from the moment I saw her, my brain just couldn't let her go.

Fuck. I don't know what to do.

There's nothing to do, you asshole. You're in love with her. It's too late.

When I brought Sydney to the clubhouse tonight, I watched her like a spy. Like I was pretending to be invisible. To see her — all of her — as though I wasn't there.

What I saw was a woman who looked happy. Happy to be there. Happy to be with me. A woman who might have run away from a tough past, but who trusted me to open up to about all of it.

And fuck. I trust her, too, I realize. Shit, I do. As much as I've told myself in the past to never trust a woman. To never let myself get stupid about one. God help me, but I've gone against my one cardinal rule. I can't fucking believe it, but there it is.

I finally think I understand what Ghost and Hawk have with Jenna and Sam. What makes Ghost's eyes change when he looks at Jenna. What makes Hawk smile at Sam like he never smiles at anyone else.

Sydney's not like Rob Sims' cheating bitch of a widow. I can't believe she could ever be like that. She's not like my mom was with my dad.

I don't know if Sydney could ever love me. But I want to believe she can.

And I want to believe it's the kind of love I could be worthy of.

29
SYDNEY

The next morning, the air is crisp and fresh, and after the rainstorm the night before, everything looks bright and new. I spend the whole next day at Gavin's lake house. Since it's Sunday, the Golden Cup is closed, so I have an entire, glorious day with nothing to do but laze in bed with him, make love, talk, and eat when we realize we're absolutely starving. He convinces me to spend the next night there with him, too — though I don't need very much convincing — and the following morning, he drives me back to my house in time for work.

I'm deliciously sore from him, my entire body alive with the memory of his touch as I open the shop. It's a typical Monday morning, except that this morning I'm feeling exceptionally lazy and can't stop wishing that I was still lying in bed with Gavin instead of here serving customers and making espresso drinks.

Things between the two of us feel… *different* somehow, after this weekend. I don't know if I'm imagining it, but Gavin is more tender with me. More open, too. He told me stories about him and Gunner in the Marines, stories that made me laugh so hard I was snorting. He told me some other things, too, like how he lived in a home with alcoholic parents and an abusive father. How when he was eleven, his father shot and wounded a man, landing him in prison. That his mom was unfit to care for him and his sister Kessa, and so the state put them into foster care. How he decided early on that the only one that could take care of him was himself. And how, to do that, he relied on the only thing he learned from his dad: how to fight.

Gavin told me a little more about the problems the Lords of Carnage are facing, too. Not a lot. Only that it's dangerous at the moment, and that he'll do everything in his power to keep it all away from me. He tells me I'm safe, that he'll never let anyone do anything to hurt me.

And I don't doubt that for one second. Not at all.

What about *him*, though?

Gavin's told me that he'll be busy with club business most of this week, and warned me that he might not be able to see me as much as he'd like until a few things get taken care of. Still, for some reason I keep half-expecting him to stop by the shop this morning on his way to the clubhouse or wherever. As the minutes tick by, then turn to hours, and he still doesn't show, I start to get agitated. And then I get pissed at myself for being more disappointed than I have any right to be.

I'm refilling milk and cream dispensers and berating myself for being such a needy idiot when the front door opens. Looking up expectantly, my pulse speeds to a flutter.

It's not Gavin. My heart drops in disappointment. But it *is* someone I recognize, though for a second I can't place her.

"Sydney!" she waves. Her voice, and her long, dark brown hair, finally snap into place who it is.

"Sam!" I say in surprise. "Hey, what are you doing here?"

Sam flashes me a wide grin. "Just thought I'd come in and check out your shop. I've been meaning to come in for a while now, actually. But now I can say I know the owner!"

She's not alone. Holding her hand is a little boy of about three years old. He's blond, with enormous blue eyes that seem to take in everything at once. I step out from behind the counter to greet them.

"This is Connor," she says, looking down at the boy. "Connor, this is Sydney."

I crouch down so that I'm at eye level with him. "Hi, Connor. Pleased to meet you." He looks at me solemnly with his wide eyes, and moves to hide behind Sam's leg. I make a goofy face at him. He hesitates for a moment, sizing me up, then ducks his head shyly and smiles.

"Connor, let's see if we can find you something yummy to eat in that case over there, okay?" Sam says to him. Connor nods and allows himself to be led to the pastry case, and Sam starts to tell him what each of the items are. Eventually, he points at the chocolate muffins, and I go behind the counter and pull one out for him.

"I'd love a hot chocolate," Sam says. "And a glass of milk for him."

I get their drinks and ring her up. Since there's no one else waiting to be served, I come with them as they settle into a table not far from the counter and decide to sit down with them for a few minutes.

"I didn't realize you and Hawk had a child," I say as I drop into a chair.

"Oh, we don't. I mean," she laughs, "Connor isn't his or mine, biologically. We're his foster parents. For now, anyway." She takes Connor's muffin and pulls the paper off for him, then sets it back on his plate. "We've applied to adopt him, and we're just waiting to hear whether our application has been accepted."

"Wow." I'm impressed. "Is it looking good for you that they'll say yes? I hear adoption can be really complicated."

"It's a long process," she agrees. "But in Connor's case, his biological family is supportive of our taking him. So we're hoping it will go smoothly."

I look over at the little boy, who is happily munching on a bit of muffin, his mouth already dark with chocolate. My heart melts just a little.

"He's a sweetheart, isn't he?" Sam says, reading my thoughts. "We love him so, so much. Hawk and I started fostering him pretty early on in our relationship, so he's been with us for almost as long as we've been together. I can't imagine our lives without him."

"He's a doll." My mind tries to wrap itself around Hawk as a dad. It seems so incongruous to imagine a big, tough, tattooed biker as a father. Then again, Jenna told me that she and Ghost have two kids of their own, and apparently Ghost dotes on them even more than she does.

"So." Sam leans back with a conspiratorial smirk on her face. "Change of subject. You and Brick. Spill."

I can't help but snort at her directness. "Um. Spill?" I stammer, stalling for time. "Like, what?"

"You know!" she wiggles her eyebrows suggestively. "What's he like in…" She glances over at Connor. "During… *playtime?*"

I redden, and try to think how to respond. "He's really, *really* good at… *playing*," I finally manage.

"I bet," she smirks. "Has he asked you to be his old lady yet?"

"Old lady?" I wrinkle my nose at the term.

Sam laughs. "It does sound kind of weird, I know. But that's what the guys in the MC call their girlfriends and wives. It means you're his, and his alone. Forever. Off limits to all the other men."

"Oh," I say, reddening. "No, we haven't…"

Then it hits me. A memory from our first night at the lake house.

"You're mine," he growls. "Say it."

Does he want me like that? Is that what he meant?

A little shiver runs through me. It's a little scary to think about, so early on. But it also makes my heart flutter in my chest.

"We haven't… really gotten that far," I say uncertainly.

"Really?" she eyes me skeptically. "Because the way he was looking at you at the clubhouse the other night, it sure seems like he's thinking about it. Hell, Hawk says he's never even seen Brick show more than a passing interest in any woman, except for… well, you know. *Playtime.*" Connor looks up at her curiously, then continues eating. "He was clearly introducing you tp us for a reason. Bringing you into the family, so to speak."

The little flutter in my chest grows to a hammering. Because the fact is? As crazy as it seems, I'm hoping she's right about this. I realize now as I sit here, the last couple of days with Gavin have been the happiest I can ever remember being. By a long shot. I want it to continue. I want us to continue. I *want* to be his.

"Sam," I murmur, deciding to ask her a question that's been on my mind all morning. "Brick was telling me this weekend about some trouble that's happening with the club. Do you know anything about that?"

She nods. "Yeah. Hawk's told me. Not the details, of course. The men keep the club business strictly to themselves. But I know from what he's told me that it concerns a rival club, and I think it has something to do with some of the crimes that have been happening here in Tanner Springs."

Connor has finished his muffin now, and he climbs down from his chair and comes to sit in Sam's lap. She pulls him up and grabs a napkin to wipe off his mouth. "It can be a little nerve wracking, when you know something's up with the club. That's just a reality of being in this life. But I trust Hawk, and I know he'll do everything he can to keep his brothers safe, and us out of danger." She looks at me. "You should trust Brick, too. He's a good man, and he'll do anything to protect the people he cares about."

"I do," I say, and I realize it's true. I trust Gavin completely. Ultimately, I'd trust him with my life. I know instinctively that he would throw himself in front of a bullet for me. Hell, he's been trying to protect me from the very beginning, from threats I didn't even know about.

For the first time since my father died, I feel like there's someone out there who accepts me for who I am, and whose only agenda is to try to protect me and keep me safe.

I'm not used to this. My whole life, I've been taught that the only person I can rely on is myself. Even my father taught me to keep my cards close to my chest, because in our world, the more someone knows about you, the more they can use that knowledge against you.

I've been holding myself back from Gavin. Telling him only half of my story. Partly from fear, and partly from habit. But if things continue down the path I think they're on — if Gavin bringing me to meet his people means what Sam says it means…

If he feels the same way about me that I'm starting to feel about him…

Then it's time for me to put my trust in him.

It's time for me to tell Gavin the whole story of why Syd Banner really left Atlantic City.

30
BRICK

The last week, things have really heated up. The MC has been increasing our "patrolling" — making the rounds of area businesses, talking to their owners and trying to catch any criminal activity before it starts. We're on rotating rounds twenty-four seven and we're stretched thin as hell. I've barely seen Sydney in days, and the only silver lining is, I'm usually too tired for my cock to protest much about it.

All the Lords are assembled in the chapel, for the first time since we decided as a club to go after Black. Tweak's been working even harder than the rest of us, and has managed to locate the Spiders' clubhouse and get a video camera system ready so that a group of the men can go down there incognito and set them up. We're hoping to get as much intel as we need on the Iron Spiders and Black's activity to make a move within the next week.

"I need some volunteers to go into Spiders territory and case the clubhouse and grounds and place the cameras," Rock growls. Pretty much all the hands go up, including mine. He looks around the table. "Not Brick, or Ghost. I'm saving you two for the actual hit. You'll be coming with me for that."

"You sure it makes sense for you to go?" Angel asks, turning to him. "If we send the head of our club to take out the head of their club, we risk weakening ourselves if the hit goes bad. We need our prez in place, strong, no matter what happens. Why don't I go in your place?"

"He's got a point, Rock," Geno rumbles from the other side of the table. "Sending Angel makes more sense. He's…"

"I go," Rock says sharply. "This is *my* fuckin' war. Black is threatening my club. He's mine to take out."

Silence fills the air. No one's going to challenge Rock on this, though it's clear from the looks on a few of the brothers' faces they don't agree with his decision.

"Sarge, Thorn, Tweak, and Striker," Rock barks. "You'll take one of the cages. Set up the cameras, find a place with good cover to watch the clubhouse from. Report back to me once you've got everything in place."

"We gonna set up shifts to watch them?" Thorn asks. "Or let the cameras do their work?"

Rock is about to respond when a tentative knock interrupts him. Gunner glances at me with a frown. All eyes turn to the chapel door. It's got to be one of the women, and all of them know better than to knock during church. Or ever, for that matter. The chapel is off limits to everyone who isn't a patched member of the Lords.

Thorn stands and turns the knob, pulling the door open. On the other side is Jewel. She looks nervously around at us, her face pale.

"I'm sorry," she half-whispers. "The mayor is here. He wants to see you, Rock. He said either you come out right now or you'll be seeing the inside of a jail cell before the day is through."

"Goddamnit," Rock seethes. "All right. Meeting adjourned. For now." He bangs the gavel on the table and stands. We follow him out of the room, and into the main area of the clubhouse.

Jarred Holloway is standing there with Chief Crup, both of them looking as out of place as nuns in a whore house.

"You damn well better have a warrant," Rock says in a low, menacing voice as he walks toward them. The rest of us stop and stand in a rough formation behind him.

"We're not searching your place today, Rock," Holloway answers. "But I doubt you're gonna think that's a good thing when we're done."

"What the fuck are you here for, then?"

"Your club's finally gone too far, Antony," Crup spits.

"What the hell does that mean?"

Crup lets out a snort of derision. "Okay. We'll play that game. I don't suppose your club knows anything about the gas fire at Lloyd's Automotive."

"No, afraid we don't," Rock answers him. "Is there some reason you came in person to let us know this?"

"Someone who lives in the neighborhood told the police this morning that they saw some guys in leather vests creeping around there last night." Crup's eyes narrow in contempt.

"Why the fuck would we set fire to Lloyd's?" Ghost challenges him.

"Seems pretty obvious to me," Crup says. "A rival business to your garage, the one *legitimate* business you have going?"

"Oh, fucking come *on*," Angel half-shouts. "Jesus, that's fucking ridiculous."

"And this time, you've really screwed the pooch," Holloway continues. "Steve Lloyd's in the hospital. Second and third degree burns. Got trapped inside trying to put out the fire."

"Jesus fuck," Gunner swears under his breath, shaking his head. "Poor fucking Lloyd."

Gunner went to high school with Steve Lloyd, I know. Hell, they still get together from time to time to go fishing.

"The Lords had nothing to do with that fire, Holloway," Rock growls. "We don't shit where we live."

Holloway snorts. "Why would I believe the word of a criminal, Rock? Especially over the eyewitness testimony of a fine upstanding citizen of Tanner Springs, who said he saw *your* men at the scene of the crime just before the fire?"

"That's not possible," Ghost growls.

"You sure your 'witness' isn't just seeing what he wants to see?" Angel says sardonically.

Holloway shakes his head and continues talking to Rock as though Ghost and Angel haven't even spoken. "I'm sorry, Rock," he says in a voice tinged with fake regret, "but the people of this town expect me to do what I was elected to do." He takes a step forward. "A word to the wise — and I certainly hope you *are* wise enough to heed it. Shut this club down, or move out of Tanner Springs." He pauses. "Or we'll do it for you."

Without waiting for an answer, Holloway turns and walks toward the exit. Crup follows. When they're gone, Rock goes into the chapel by himself and slams the door.

"Shit," mutters Angel. "This is the last fucking thing we need right now."

I don't say anything. I know Holloway well enough to know he's more than capable of trumping up charges that could put enough of us behind bars to force the club out. If anything more happens that can be pinned on the club, I have no doubt he'd act on his threat.

"We need to move now on taking out Black," Angel says. Next to us, Geno grunts his agreement.

"We can't afford any mistakes on that front," I mutter. Angel looks over and meets my eyes. He nods once, and then looks away. We're both thinking the same thing, I know: he'd be a better choice than Rock as part of the team that goes to do the job.

Geno clears his throat. "I could sure as hell use a smoke," he says to us. "You two feel like joining me?"

Outside, the three of us light up and stand in silence for a few moments. It seems pretty clear that Geno's brought us out here for a reason, but it's his decision to say what he wants to say in his own time. Finally, he takes a long drag on his smoke and tosses it on the ground.

"You know," he begins, "Rock, and me, and Smiley, we go way back. The three of us are the only original members of the Lords. I've known Rock since he was younger than the two of you."

Angel nods. The three older men are all in their fifties by now. All of them are starting to show their age, though except for Smiley they're still tough enough to make most men fear them.

"One day," Geno continues, "you'll be getting older, and you'll look back and realize you never saw the time pass. And then across the table, most of your brothers will be young enough to be your sons. And you'll see they're the future. And you're the past."

Angel glances at me, then at Geno, but doesn't say anything.

"It takes a big man to admit that," Geno sighs. "And an even bigger man to admit that one of these days, you're gonna have to relinquish control of something you built from the ground up." He fixes his eyes on Angel. "Admit that there's someone next in line to take your place." Geno takes another cigarette from the pack in his pocket and lights it. "And sometimes, not wanting to admit things can cloud your judgment." He takes a puff, blows it out, and then begins to chuckle. "Like last week when I decided I could saw down and remove a tree branch that fell on my roof by myself, instead of hiring someone else to come and do it. Damn near broke my neck."

"We're not talking about your tree branch, are we?" Angel says. It's not really a question.

"Nope," Geno agrees. "I've been noticing the two of you chafing at some of Rock's decisions lately. And I'm here to say I don't blame you. But I also want to tell you I know Rock pretty damn well. And I wouldn't be surprised if he's fighting with himself, knowing sooner or later he's gonna need to step down, but not feeling ready yet." He looks at Angel. "And he sees you're ready to step up. You're gonna be a good, strong president, Angel. We can all see that. Rock included." He sighs. "But that doesn't mean it's easy to accept, when you're used to being the leader yourself."

We stay outside for a few more minutes, each of us lost in our own thoughts. Eventually, we head back into the clubhouse, passing Gunner on his way out. He tells us he's going to the hospital to see Steve and his wife Michelle.

"I don't know if they're gonna want to see me," he says, his face grim. "But I need them to know it wasn't our club that did this. Even if no one else in town believes it, I want to make sure they do."

Back inside, Ghost tells us that Rock's gone upstairs to his apartment. Any further discussion about our hit on Black will wait until tomorrow, when Sarge, Thorn, and the others are back from their run into Spiders territory. Meantime, the other brothers have turned their attention to letting off some steam. From the look of things, there's gonna be more than a few hung over Lords tomorrow.

Ghost hands me a bottle of beer, but I wave him off and check the time on my phone. It's just about closing time at the Golden Cup. More than anything right now, I want to see Sydney. I want to take her back to my place and lose myself inside her. I tell Ghost I'll see him tomorrow and head out to my bike with a smile starting to twitch at the corners of my mouth, in spite of all the shit going on around me. Instead of calling Sydney, I decide I'll just show up and surprise her. I can already hear her giving me shit about stalking her, but I know she'll be thrilled.

As I fire up the bike and pull out of the parking lot, my cock is already signaling its approval of my plan. Hell, maybe I'll give her a repeat of our first time in her office, before I take her back home and fuck her every different way I can think of until the sun comes up.

31
SYDNEY

Days pass, and just like Gavin warned me, I hardly see him because of whatever club business he's involved in.

He's away from Tanner Springs a fair bit, doing what I don't know. Often, he comes back to town so late that he decides to just sleep at one of the apartments in the clubhouse. He's good about texting me so on those days I know not expect him, but it's still hard.

We do manage to slip in a few nights together — which he jokingly calls "conjugal visits" — so at least I can carry the memory of his body with me to work in the mornings sometimes. Our lovemaking is intense and passionate, and afterwards, we both fall into an exhausted sleep. When I wake in the mornings, Gavin is usually already getting dressed, and heads out the door even before I have to leave to open up the coffee shop.

We see so little of each other that I never quite find the time to bring up the texts from Devon like I planned to. Or tell Gavin about the details of how and why I left Atlantic City. I don't want to waste what little time we have together, so I tell myself I'll wait until his crisis with the MC has passed and then I'll tell him the whole story. Sometimes, lying awake in his arms, listening to his breathing as he sleeps, I feel a pang of guilt, but I push it away. Gavin's got enough on his mind. I'm not sure what's happening with the club, but whatever it is, I want him to be focused on keeping himself safe right now, not on worrying about me.

One afternoon, about a week and a half after the first night I spent with him at his lake house, I'm at the Golden Cup, trying to keep my mind off how much I miss Gavin. It's late afternoon, and Hailey is here working. Her crush, Teddy, is sitting at a small table against the wall by the condiment station, doing homework. Every ten minutes or so, Hailey will go over to him and they'll engage in some obvious flirting, with her tossing back her hair and laughing at his jokes like he's the funniest person she's ever met. And right now, he probably is.

Maybe it should bug me that she's kind of shirking on the job, but it's actually sort of sweet. And anyway, she doesn't do it when there are customers waiting, so it's not yet to the level where I feel like I have to reprimand her.

"So…" I murmur in a low voice, after one of her trips to his table. "What's up with the two of you? Are you going out yet?"

"No, not yet," she tells me, her face turning pink. "We're just friends. I don't even know if he likes me *that way.*"

"Oh, please," I laugh. "Hailey, he's sitting in this shop, by himself, doing his homework while you're working. He's only here because you are. There's no other reason he'd be here."

"Her eyes widen hopefully. "Do you think so?" she asks. *Oh, my gosh, was I ever this young?* I wonder.

"Yes, I do." I glance over at Teddy, and catch him staring our way. When he sees me looking at him, he hastily puts his head down and pretends to concentrate on his homework. "So relax. He likes you. Enjoy it."

She leans toward me conspiratorially. "I think he might ask me to homecoming," she whispers.

"I think he might, too," I grin.

A customer comes in then, and I let Hailey serve him while I go in the back and check that the bathroom doesn't need cleaning or restocking. She's just ringing him up when I come back out.

"Hailey, I've been meaning to ask you," I say. "Do you happen to know any reliable kids your age who might want to work here? The shop's getting busy enough that I think it's time for me to hire some more people."

Honestly, I probably should have done this a couple of months ago. It's getting to the point that at our busiest times, it's almost too much for one person to handle. But I've held off until now because until recently, it never bothered me to work long hours. Now, though…

Well, as much as I hate to admit it, the prospect of having a little more free time is definitely starting to sound appealing. Especially because that would mean I'd have more time to see Gavin, once he's dealt with his club problem. It makes me feel sort of silly to think in those terms. I've never rearranged my life for a relationship before. But having Gavin in my life has made me realize how little of a social life I've given myself since I moved to Tanner Springs.

Now, I'm sort of hoping that that might change. Already, Sam's been back to the coffee shop, this time with Jenna, and the two of them asked me if I'd want to come out with them sometime for drinks and dinner.

Hailey tilts her head, considering my question. "I think so. Yeah. At least one, that I can think of right now. One of my friends is saving up money to go on a class trip to Paris for spring break. I bet she'd be interested. I'll ask around."

"Thanks." It would be great if I could manage to get some good workers through Hailey. She's a good kid, and her friends, from what I've seen of them, seem pretty level-headed as well.

Teddy comes up to the counter then. "Hey," he nods to Hailey, looking at her through his curtain of black bangs. "My mom just texted me. She wants me to come home for dinner. My dad's been gone on a work trip for the last week, and he just got back."

"Oh, okay," Hailey says, looking disappointed.

"Hey. You could come for dinner, if you want," he says suddenly.

"Wouldn't your mom mind?" Hailey asks. She's trying in vain to keep the excitement out of her voice.

"Nah. My mom would be cool with it. She's always okay with friends eating over. She just wants us all there tonight, is all."

Hailey opens her mouth to respond, and then looks over at me. "Oh. That'd be cool, but... I'm supposed to work until close tonight."

I probably shouldn't do it, but I just *can't* be the reason Hailey doesn't get to go over to Teddy's house for dinner.

"It's fine," I say, waving my hand at her. "I can close up tonight."

"Are you sure?" Hailey looks like she can't believe I'm doing this. "I mean..."

"It's really no problem." I smile at her. "Things are kind of slow right now, anyway. I bet I can get most of it done before closing time."

Teddy goes to pack up his stuff. Hailey gives me an excited grin and mouths "Thank you!" at me as she hops off to go grab her backpack from the back.

"I owe you like a million!" she whispers to me when she comes back. Teddy's by the door now, waiting for her.

"All I expect is a full report," I murmur. "And find me some employees."

"Done!" Hailey hops off, a cute little skip in her step, and follows Teddy out of the shop. I watch as the two of them get into his car and drive away. *Ah, young love…*

As I predicted, it continues to be a slow late afternoon and evening, and I'm able to get a lot of the closing stuff done while the shop is still open. By the time I flip over the closed sign and lock the door, all I still have to do is clean the bathroom, take out the trash, and do a quick sweep of the floors. I decide to do the bathroom last, because that's the job I hate the most. So I grab the broom and sweep the front, then dump the debris in the large garbage can I keep by the counter. Tying off the full bag, I lug it to the back, kick open the back door, and move the heavy cinder block I leave back there, to keep the door propped open so it doesn't lock behind me.

I make it to the dumpster, throw the bag in, and go back inside. I put a fresh bag in the large bin, then move on to the other, smaller ones, combining them into one large bag, which I haul out as well. When I'm back inside, I'm about to kick the cinder block away when I realize I forgot the trash can in the bathroom.

I'm walking back down the hall, wondering if I can get away with just scrubbing the toilet before I leave, when a sudden movement to my left startles me. Before I can turn to see what it is, I'm slammed roughly against the wall, a hand wrapping around my throat.

"I believe," Devon says in a low, menacing voice, "that I asked you where the hell's my money?"

32
SYDNEY

I'm so shocked that I don't even have time to cry out. The only sound that manages to escape is a small choking sound when I feel the hard metallic jut of a gun barrel against the sensitive skin of my throat.

"Did you really fucking think you could escape me?" Devon rasps through clenched teeth. "Did you really think I wouldn't track you down? I've been watching you, you know. Biding my time."

His grasp around my throat is so painfully tight I'm having trouble breathing, even through my nose. I'm clutching wildly at the wall, trying to find some purchase so I can pull away, but there's nothing.

I can't breathe. *Is he here to kill me? Is this really it? Do I die here?* My brain tries to form coherent thoughts, to keep my panic from taking control of me.

Devon is pressed close against me now, his body pinning me against the wall. Through the fabric of his pants, I can feel that he's hard. "I'm taking my hand away now," he mutters. "Don't scream. Are we clear?" Wide-eyed, I nod as much as I'm able. Slowly, he releases my throat. I gasp, taking in desperate lungfuls of air. Tears spring to my eyes.

He pulls the gun from my throat and takes a step away, training it on me as he watches me trying to catch my breath. His face is a mixture of lust and hatred.

"I've missed you, Syd," he says simply, and for a moment he sounds like the old days. "Why the fuck did you leave? Why the fuck did you have to steal from me?"

Shit. I don't know how to play this. Devon feels… volatile. I've never seen this side of him, at least not directed toward me. My mind is racing, grasping at any possible means of escape. But I can't see anything. Not yet, not while he has a gun. The only thing I can think to do is answer his questions. Tell him the truth, more or less. And try to bide my time until he gets distracted and I can try to get the weapon away from him somehow.

"Devon," I begin, forcing my voice not to quiver. "I didn't steal from you. Not really. You and I both know you were skimming money from the team. I just took back what I was owed. I didn't even take it all. Just enough to get me started someplace else."

He doesn't move for a second. I'm afraid he's going to fly into a rage. But for some reason, his face goes deadly calm.

"That money could have been both of ours, you know," he says.

I know what he means. He means, if we'd stayed together.

"I know," I reply. "But..." I stop, realizing I need to choose my words very carefully. "But I had never been on my own, Devon. All my life, I was my dad's little girl, and then on your team. I never got to choose the life I led." I take a deep breath. I'm hoping this will work. "I needed to be on my own for a while. To know whether the life I had in Atlantic City was the right one for me."

It's not a complete lie. But it's not far away from one.

Then I see it. In his eyes. Just the tiniest flicker. He's wondering if I mean that I was considering coming back. Right now, this is what I need him to believe. I need him to think there's a chance, so he won't hurt me.

"I knew you wouldn't approve," I say, casting my eyes down. "But I knew you'd forgive me."

The look on his face is suspicious, but I can tell my words are having an effect. If I wasn't so terrified, I'd almost find it funny, that a man who's made a career out of reading other people and exploiting their weaknesses could be so easy to read himself.

He moves closer to me again.

"And now?" he asks in a low voice.

"It's been good for me here," I tell him honestly. "It's a totally different life."

He snorts softly. "This isn't a life for people like you and me, Syd. This fucking dot on the map in flyover country? This isn't going to be enough for you. You'll never last out here."

I don't say anything.

He's close again, pressed up against me. His erection is still there. Devon raises the hand that's not holding the gun, and I'm afraid he's going to choke me again, but instead he grasps my chin, raising my face to his.

"Is there anyone else?" he asks me.

I force myself not to think about Gavin, because I know it will show on my face.

"No," I say "There's no one else."

He bends toward me then, and kisses me, his tongue searching insistently for mine. I force myself to let him, terrified that he'll know I don't want it, but he doesn't notice.

"Syd," he breathes. "Come back to Atlantic City. Come back, and we'll forget all this."

"I can't," I say, and then quickly try to soften it as I see his face begin to change. "I mean, not right away. I can't just leave the shop. It would take time." I tilt my head to the front of the store. "To sell everything, I mean. To close everything up. It would take months."

"Fuck the shop," he grunts. "I don't need the money. *We* don't need the money. We can make this kind of cash in a month." His hand moves to caress my cheek. I try not to flinch. "Walk away, Syd. Come back with me."

"I can't," I whisper.

He pulls his face away an inch or so, and looks me hard in the eyes.

"You're fucking playing me," he hisses.

He rears back, the back of his hand slapping hard against my face before I can stop it. I yelp in surprise and alarm as it connects with my jaw, the pain slicing through my thoughts.

"You're fucking playing me!" he roars. "You fucking whore, you've always been playing me with that cunt of yours."

"No!" I cry, even though I know it's too late, he's done believing me. I have to try something else. "Devon, please!" I beg him. "I'll pay you back every cent I took when I left. I promise you. Please, just let me go. Let this go. Just please, leave me alone!"

His face is becoming a mask of rage. "You think it's the money you owe me? The *money*? I fucking waited for you, like a goddamn *pussy*, instead of just taking what was mine as soon as you joined my team. Out of respect for your father, I should have known you were just fucking me to get what you wanted out of me, like the little whore you are!" he roars. "*That* was my fucking mistake — letting you think you had a goddamn choice in the matter. You don't have a fucking choice, Syd." He grabs my wrist, twisting it painfully behind my back, and pushes me so hard toward my office that I stumble and hit my shoulder against the other wall of the hallway. "Get in there and give me what's fucking mine."

No! my mind screams. *I can't let him do this. I can't let him…* I try to run, but he catches me easily and shoves me into the office. *What can I do?* I try to think of any scenario that would stop this. He has a gun. He'll have to put it down at some point… won't he? Can I try to gouge his eyes out? Knee him in the balls? Adrenaline shoots through me — it's too late for words now, I'm going to have to act, and hope for the best. He tells me to lie on the desk and spread my legs. Crazily, my thoughts turn to Gavin, and I have to stifle a sob. I feel sick, I *can't* do this…

Suddenly, Devon is flying backward, like he's been pushed back by an explosion. The hand that's holding his gun pinwheels upward. An ear-splitting bang detonates, obliterating all other sound for a second as Devon pulls the trigger and fires into the ceiling. Then he's on the ground, the gun torn from his hands by the man who begins to pistol-whip him with it.

33
BRICK

I get to the Golden Cup just a couple of minutes after closing. I'm peering through the glass of the front door to the Golden Cup, about to rap on the door so Sydney will come let me in, when I see something. Movement, in the hallway.

It's Sydney.

And she's kissing someone.

The powerful cocktail of rage, shock, and confusion that hits me almost knocks me flat on my ass. I fucking can't believe what I'm seeing. Of all the things I could ever believe about Sydney, this is dead goddamn last. And yet it's right in front of me.

My first instinct is to beat down the door, but I'm so fucking angry right now I'm pretty sure I'll end up killing one or both of them if I do. It takes everything I've got in me, but

I force myself to turn around and walk back down the street toward my bike.

The next few minutes are a blur. I open the throttle and speed away so fast it's a minor miracle I don't lay the bike down. I don't even know where I'm going, I just know I'm trying to drive faster than the thoughts careening around in my head and it's not working. When I run through a stoplight and almost hit a middle-aged lady on a bike, something snaps in my head and I realize I need to get off the bike before I kill someone, so I pull into the gravel parking lot of a shuttered crafts store and start pacing instead.

Sydney.

How could I have not seen this in her?

How in the fuck did I ever get in so deep with her that it's ripping me to shreds like this? How the fuck did I let myself fall in love with her, like a goddamn idiot?

Jesus fucking Christ. I pace faster, clenching and unclenching my fists, unable to stop. I need a goddamn wall to punch. I need something to hit. To *destroy.*

It's unbelievable. It's impossible. It's fucking *impossible.*

It's...

Kind of impossible.

The seed of a doubt starts to form in my head, stopping me in my crazed tracks.

Everything in me tells me Sydney wouldn't do this. That's what's fucking with my head so much. Even after *seeing* it, I'm still having a hard time believing it.

But I did see it. And I *know* what I saw.

Don't I?

Do I?

I don't know why the idea suddenly clicks inside my head just then. I almost can't make myself do it, but I have to know. With an unsteady hand, I reach back and pull my cell phone out of my pocket, walking over to a shaded area to the side so I can see the screen better. I fumble through the apps until I find the ones that connect to the security cams I installed at the Golden Cup, and click on the one that shows me the front of the shop and the hallway. I slide the bar with my finger to move the video back twenty minutes, and start fast-forwarding through.

And roar with rage when I see the man throw Sydney against the wall, his hand around her throat.

The minutes it takes me to get back are the longest of my fucking life. I'm sick with fear, convinced I'm too late to stop whatever he's about to do to her. Instead of going to the front, I fly into the alley and drop my bike in the small lot next to her car, which at least is still there. I reach into the waistband of my pants for my gun in preparation to shoot the lock off the back door, but when I get there, it's *open,* propped ajar with a cinder block. I don't assess the situation like I should, I just fling open the fucking door, and they're not in the hallway anymore, but when I round the corner to Sydney's office she's there on the desk and this motherfucker is pointing a revolver at her and it's obvious what's about to happen.

I reach up and yank him back by the hair, throwing him down onto the floor. His finger was on the trigger so it goes off, missing me by about a foot as the bullet lodges in the ceiling. I wrench the revolver out of his grasp, ignoring the yelp of pain as I bend his wrist back violently. Then I'm down on the floor, the gun in my hand, and I'm going to kill him with it eventually but right now I just want to beat on him, so I smash the handle against his face, again and again, enjoying the crunch of his nose as it breaks and the spurt of blood and the gurgling sound as he struggles to scream and breathe.

"Gavin! No!"

At first, her voice seems far away, almost like I'm dreaming it.

"Gavin, please! Please, don't kill him!" She's down on the ground with me now, grabbing at my arm and trying to make me stop hitting him.

I stop what I'm doing, putting a hand around his throat in a vise-like grip and look at her uncomprehendingly.

"Please!" She's panting, her eyes wide. "Don't kill him!"

"Why the hell not?" I manage to say through the fog of my rage.

"I… I don't want you to go to prison." Her eyes fill with tears. "Please, *please* let him go!"

"Who is he?" I demand.

"His name is Devon," she tells me. She's pale, frightened. "He was the leader of the team I was on in Atlantic City." Sydney glances at him, and then quickly away. "When I left, I didn't tell him. I took some money that belonged to me and walked away. I thought he'd let me go, but…" She shakes her head. "Somehow he found out I was living here in Tanner Springs. He… he found my phone number, and texted me a couple of times, but I didn't think…" A strangled sob breaks from her throat. Her hand goes to her face, and she takes a few deep breaths to calm herself. "I didn't really think he would come for me."

If Sydney wanted to make an argument for me not killing him, that wasn't it.

"Please," she whispers, as though she can read my thoughts.

I look down at the hamburgered mess of the motherfucker's face. He's barely struggling right now, and I think it's because he's having trouble breathing.

"I will kill you next time," I tell him. "Know that. If you ever come back to this town again. If you ever come near her. Fuck, if you ever leave New Jersey. I will end you."

His eyes are wide and terrified. I ease up slightly on his windpipe.

"Yes," he gasps.

I stand up, and for good measure land one good kick into his abdomen with my boot. He doubles over and begins to retch. Beside me, Sydney flinches.

"Crawl your fucking ass out of here," I spit. "If you're not gone in ten seconds, get ready for another round."

Impassively, I watch as he claws at the floor and drags himself through the hallway and out the back door. I kick the cinder block away and the door shuts behind him.

I come back to where Sydney is standing. She flings herself into my arms and begins to cry.

"Oh, my God," she sobs against my chest. "Gavin, thank God! He… he was going to…"

"I know," I murmur. "I saw what he was going to do."

"I never thought he'd… I mean, I thought he was just trying to scare me. I thought… I don't know… that he'd get tired of it when I didn't respond."

"And you never thought to tell me," I say.

"I didn't think it was a big deal at the time," she sighs. "I was going to tell you, but I didn't want you to worry about me. I just thought you'd go into over-protective mode. I was going to wait until your club business stuff was over, so you could focus on that."

"And now, instead," I continue, "I just have to worry about you lying to me."

"What? Oh, come on, Gavin!" she cries, pulling back to look up at me. "I didn't lie to you! I just…" she stops, stricken. "I just…"

"Didn't tell me the truth," I finish for her.

"I was going to tell you" she half-wails. "But I didn't want you to overreact!"

"Over-fucking-*react?*" I yell in disbelief. "What exactly would have been overreacting about the fact that some ex-boyfriend of yours was going to try to *kill* you?"

"I don't think he would have killed me," she protests weakly. "He just… wanted…" Her voice trails off, her lip trembling. "He…"

I know *exactly* what he fucking wanted. The murderous rage is back, and I have to stop myself from storming out the back door and putting a bullet in his goddamn skull.

The fury is so overwhelming that it almost feels like a physical force inside me, fighting to get out.

Then, just like that, it's gone.

"I've been trying to keep you safe since we met," I say. My voice sounds flat, and kind of far away. "I thought you were worth it. I fucking cared about you." I look at her. "And you couldn't even be bothered to tell me this. You couldn't be bothered to let me in enough to know where the real threats were."

"It's not like that at all!" she screams. "I was trying to protect you!"

"I don't need protecting, Sydney," I say, detaching myself from her. "What I need is to be able to trust you. Which I can't. Not anymore."

It feels like all the adrenaline has drained out of my body at once. Suddenly, I don't feel anything but dead inside.

Mechanically, I walk over to the back door and open it. That motherfucker Devon is long gone.

"Get in your car," I command.

"Gavin, I —"

"Get in your car!" I roar. "Now!"

Frightened, she goes into her office, grabs her purse, and does as she's told. I slam the door behind both of us.

"Go home," I tell her. "Lock the door."

"Gavin," she says tentatively, tears in her eyes. "Are you… coming over?"

"No." I walk over to where I dumped my bike on the ground, and haul it upright. "We're done, Sydney. That way, you don't ever have to lie to me again."

She calls my name over the sound of my bike, but I don't turn around.

I don't know where I'm going, but I can't be here anymore.

34
BRICK

It's been a week since I walked out of Sydney's coffee shop.

I haven't seen her. I haven't responded to any of her texts.

I've barely slept. Or eaten.

I've drunk enough whiskey for a small army.

I've only been back to the lake house once, for a change of clothes. I can't be there right now. Sydney fucking ruined that place for me. It was the only place I really felt at home. My sanctuary.

Now I'm thinking about selling it.

Or burning it to the ground.

I've not always had an easy time of it. My home life was shit when I was a kid. I got separated from my sister and put in foster care when I was eleven. I did a stint in juvie at sixteen. Joined the Marines at eighteen. I learned to live with very little in the way of possessions, or human contact, or family.

But I don't think I've ever felt as dead inside as I feel right now.

The fucked up thing is, I'd opened my cold, atrophied heart up to Sydney more than I ever realized it. It was like I'd lived my whole life in black and white and shades of gray, and she gave me this glimpse into a world full of color, that was right there all the time, but I never knew it.

I let myself hope it was real. Like a fucking pussy.

And now I'm back in the black and white world. Only because of her, instead of just being reality, now it feels like hell.

* * *

Tweak has been working hard, doing his magic, and he's found the intel on where the Spiders' clubhouse is. It's on a dirt and gravel road several miles outside of town. No neighbors or other buildings around, well isolated from the main road.

Tweak's showing us photos of the clubhouse and area now, on a large screen against the far wall of the chapel. The clubhouse itself is a pole building, probably about eight-thousand square feet, on a plot of land that looks to be a couple acres or so. A pitted gravel parking lot surrounds the building, and it's large enough that it serves as an effective barrier to entry, because the complete absence of cover means anyone approaching the building from any side would be immediately noticed.

"We've got video cams on the clubhouse and also on the gravel road," he tells us. He clicks on his laptop to the surveillance footage streaming from the camera that's trained on the clubhouse, so we can see what he's talking about. The cam is positioned far away, as it has to be, but he zooms up onto the building as he talks until he gets a fairly decent image closer up. At the moment, there's no sign of life. The building looks deserted except for some tire tracks made in the mud after a recent rain. "There are three loading bays on the other side of the building," Tweak explains. "Most of the time they drive their vehicles inside, so there's no evidence anyone's there."

Tweak flips the screen to another camera, which shows a long gravel road with bushes and some tree cover on either side. "This is the only way in and out," he explains. "That's a plus for us. This camera is about a mile away from their clubhouse. Close enough that we'll be able to get into position when we see from the other cam that they're leaving, and far enough away that anyone outside the clubhouse won't hear a scuffle unless there's gunshots."

Angel snorts. "Those dumb fuckers did us a favor, choosing an out of the way hellhole with only one entry point."

"We've been keeping track of Black's comings and goings," Striker pipes up. "The bastard's usually pretty well guarded, but every couple of days, he takes off with just a couple of men. We haven't tracked where he goes yet, but we have noticed that when he's on his own, he turns right onto the main highway, in the opposite direction of town."

"All right," Rock mutters. "Easiest course of action is to ambush him with the least number of men, of course. What can you give me on when you think his next least guarded trip out might be?"

"I'd be guessing Thursday," Thorn says. "Failing that, Friday."

"All right." Rock looks around. "Thursday. We head out, prepared to take out Black, and his two bodyguards if we have to. Brick, Ghost, Thorn, Gunner. You're with me on bikes. Tweak, Sarge, Striker, Tank, you'll take a van out, park on the main road and stay in contact in case we need backup."

I don't glance over at Angel, but I know he's pissed.

Geno clears his throat. "The rest of us?" he asks.

"I want all the brothers here at the MC," Rock says. "Be prepared to take action. Be prepared for lockdown, if it comes to it. Angel's in charge here *while I'm gone*."

For the first time since we started planning this, it occurs to me: if this goes south, Angel could end up president of the club. What we're doing could land any of the five of us dead.

And with Angel at the helm, the club will survive. No question.

As much as I've questioned Rock's decisions lately, and as pissed off as I know Angel is, I have to admit this is the right decision.

"Church is adjourned," Rock says. "Meet here on Thursday at oh seven-hundred. Be ready to rock and roll."

* * *

Two days later, the brothers are all assembled outside the clubhouse. I'm armed as much as I can comfortably be on the bike, with my Glock in a belt holster, three full clips in the left inside pocket of my cut, and a smaller profile Beretta in an ankle holster.

The atmosphere among the brothers is tense, but also excited. These are all men who've never backed down from a fight. In spite of the danger, you'd almost think from looking at them that they were on their way to a party instead of potentially a bloodbath.

I've killed before. I've killed enough men that I'd have to think about it if someone asked me how many. I've never had a taste for it, like some men get, but unlike some other men,

I've never had a particular problem with it if it needs to be done. I don't go into this run with any particular emotion, except grim determination to keep my brothers safe and accomplish our mission. One way or another, this is Black's last day on earth.

If it's mine, too, then so be it.

We take back roads and an out of the way route towards the Iron Spiders clubhouse, so it's less likely someone will see us and tip them off. I keep my mind resolutely off Sydney as we ride, which is harder than it sounds. Even though I'm completely done with her, she's been in my head fucking constantly since the last time I saw her. At night, when I manage to catch a rare couple of hours of sleep, it's her I dream about. Sometimes, I'm sinking myself inside her, and it's as real as if I'm actually there with her. And then I wake up in my apartment at the clubhouse, my cock as hard as iron, and I have to drink myself back to sleep so I won't give in and stroke myself to completion with her name on my lips. During the day, I vacillate between yelling at her in my head and wishing I could turn back time and give her another chance to tell me the truth.

Another chance to lie to me.

To betray me.

At least, I tell myself, *this way I'm not worried about how Sydney will react if I die today. No one will go to her like I went to Tina Sims, to tell her I'm gone. She won't be expected to pretend that it matters to her.*

Better to be alone. Better to be alone, like I've always been. For everyone's sake.

Two hours later, Rock, Ghost, Thorn, Gunner and I are all in place. In the van, Tweak, Sarge, Striker, and Tank are watching the main road and waiting instructions. Tweak's monitoring the cameras and giving us updates.

The wait is long. I smoke cigarette after cigarette, and try not to go out of my mind. Even in the Marines, the waiting before a battle was the part that always got to me. Eventually, my stomach starts to grumble, but I ignore it.

Then, suddenly, we're in motion.

Tweak's voice comes over my headset. "They're just leaving the compound. Three bikes. The one in the front is Black."

"Get ready to play ball," Ghost mutters, crouching into position.

We hear them before we see them. A triangle of three bikes, with Black front and center. From my spot concealed in the brush, I take aim at the closest one to me. I know Rock and Ghost are trained on Black. On the other side of the road, Thorn and Gunner are sighting their target.

When they're in range, I wait just a little longer, to give us the best shot possible. Then:

"Fire!" I yell.

I hit my target square in the chest. The bike closest to me drops. The man on the other side sees him, and immediately guns his engine, accelerating quickly past us. The pop-pop of gunfire sounds over the surprised shouts of the Spiders and the roar of their three engines. I get ready to move, and watch as Black reaches back for his own gun but is hit before he can get to it. His bike wobbles, but he manages to stay on, until he's hit again. He falls off backwards, the bike's momentum carrying it forward another twenty feet or so before it tips.

Rock is out of the bushes and on the road now, his gun aimed on the prone president of the Spiders. He fires three shots, then four, at Black, whose body jerks with every round. I get up and run toward him, grabbing him by the shoulder.

"Come on," I yell. "You've got him. We need to move, before the rest of them come."

We race toward our own bikes, concealed further up the road. As we run, I see that Thorn and Gunner are firing at the third Spider. One of them managed to get his rear tire, and he wobbles crazily as he tries to keep the bike from tipping, but it's a losing battle. Another bullet hits his arm, and he shrieks and topples over. As I run past him, I take aim and fire a bullet into his chest.

"Ghost! Thorn! Gunner! Move!" I shout. I'm almost at my bike now, and under the sounds of the downed motorcycles I can hear my brothers' footsteps behind me. We don't have much time now; it's a sure bet the Spiders have heard the gunfire by now. We have to be gone down the main road, before they get to Black.

"We're on our way," I hear Rock yell to Tweak and the others over the headset. "Get ready to move. You take the alternate route back."

"Copy," Tweak acknowledges. I reach my bike, fire it up, and gravel flies out from under my tires as I race toward the main road. Behind me, I hear new gunfire. I can't tell whether it's ours or theirs. Then, over the headset, I hear a cry of pain.

"Fuck! Gunner!" I shout.

"I'm hit," he yells, "But I'm okay. I'll be okay. Go!"

"Where you hit, brother?" Sarge comes over the air.

"Left thigh. I can ride like this. I'm good."

"Fuck," grits Sarge. "Not for long. Get out on the main road. Turn right toward the van and follow us until we're out of here. I'll take your bike back. We'll get you patched up best we can until we're back at the clubhouse and Smiley can take care of you."

35
BRICK

Ghost, Thorn, Rock, and I manage to get our asses out of there before the Spiders can come after us. I race back to Tanner Springs, now out of the range of headset contact with the van so I have no idea what Gunner's status is. We get back to the clubhouse in record time, but of course the van isn't there yet. I jump off the bike and immediately go find Smiley in the TV room.

"Get your shit ready," I tell him. "Gunner's hit in the thigh."

When I come back out to the main room, Rock's telling Angel what happened. I go outside and wait for the van to show up. About five minutes later, the rumble of an engine approaches, and Sarge flies in on Gunner's bike.

"They're right behind me," he barks. "Let's get ready to move Gunner."

There's a shitload of blood. Gunner's still conscious, and trying to joke around as we carry him in, but his face is pale and strained. He grits his teeth in pain when we set him down on the pool table that's been covered with large sheets of plywood.

Smiley's face is grim as he examines the wound. "He's fucking lucky it doesn't look like the bullet hit the bone at all. There's no exit wound, so the bullet's still implanted." He looks at Gunner. "I'm not gonna remove it. It's not worth it, and it could be close to a blood vessel. Taking it out I might hit something and do more harm than good."

"No worries, doc," Gunner says, giving him a tense grin. "It's not like I'm planning on setting off any metal detectors at the airport."

Smiley shoos us away from his makeshift operating table and gets to work. By now, a few of the old ladies have heard the men are back, and they're trickling in. Jenna runs to Ghost, who enfolds her in a tight embrace. Sam's over by Hawk, and I can see by her expression she's trying not to cry with relief. Geno's old lady Carmen is there, too, as is Trudy, Rock's wife, though she seems a lot calmer than the others. More years of being used to the drama and danger of being an MC prez's old lady, I guess.

For the first time since all the shooting began, I think of Sydney. I can't help but feel a pang of regret that she's not here. Though even if we were still together, I might not have told her about this run. I wouldn't have wanted her to worry.

As though she could read my mind, Sam chooses this moment to detach herself from Hawk and come over to talk to me.

"Have you called Sydney?" she asks, her voice quiet. "She'll want to know you're okay."

"We're not together anymore," I bark, a little too harshly. It's not Sam's fault, after all. "It didn't work out."

"I know," she says, her eyes reproachful. "I've seen her at the coffee shop. She's a mess, Brick."

She's not the only one. "It's a done deal. Anyway, she didn't know about any of this. So what she doesn't know can't hurt her."

I know Sydney would be right here with the rest of the other old ladies, welcoming me back, if we were still together. My mind flashes back to how natural she looked hanging out with Jenna and Sam, as if the three of them had known each other for years. My throat constricts.

"Look, Brick," Sam continues. She sounds angry. "I don't know what happened between the two of you. But I can't imagine that Sydney would ever consciously do anything to hurt you. And frankly, I can't imagine you ever doing anything to hurt her." She pauses, as though considering her words carefully. "You know," she says, "if there's one thing I've noticed about a lot of the men of the Lords of Carnage, it's that most of you are as stubborn as the day is long. You're used to getting your way, by whatever means necessary. And I think sometimes, you need the women of this club to pound some sense through your thick skulls. So I'm just gonna say this. You are most likely being an ass right now. And Sydney doesn't deserve that."

"You have no idea what you're talking about."

"No?" she challenges. "I know what it looks like when two people are in love with each other. I know what it looks like when someone's lying to himself."

"Sam," I warn. I swear to God, she's lucky she's a woman, and that she's Hawk's old lady.

"Fine," she says with a disgusted look. "I'm done. But everyone in this club can see it except you, Brick. I don't know why you'd throw away a chance at happiness."

"I'm happy," I bark, and it sounds so ridiculous that even *I* almost laugh.

"It's never as hard as stubborn people make it out to be, Brick," Sam says, and shakes her head. "All you have to do is realize it."

Fuck me. I watch her walk away, relieved as hell that this conversation is over, but now I'm just fucking angry. I go over to the bar and ask Jewel for a beer.

"Sure thing," she says, reaching for a bottle in the cooler. "By the way, how's Sydney? I haven't seen her around…"

"Not talking about it, Jewel," I cut her off with a growl. She raises her eyebrows but says nothing, and hands me my beer.

By this time, Smiley is finally finishing up on Gunner, so I head back to see him. There's a sheen of sweat on Gun's face, but he's not as pale as he was. A half-bottle of whiskey and a shot glass sit next to him. As I approach, he grabs the bottle and fills up the glass.

"Hey, there, brother." He gives me a crooked grin. "All sewn up. Smiley, you're a genius."

Smiley laughs. "Not hardly. But you keep believing that." He reaches into his bag and pulls out a small bottle of pills. "You'll want to take these to ward off the risk of infection. One pill, twice a day." He gives Gunner a pointed stare. "Try to lay off the alcohol until they're gone, too."

Gunner snorts. "Not gonna happen. But let the record show you gave me your professional medical opinion on that."

Smiley moves off, and I lean against the table and hold up my bottle to Gunner, who clinks his shot glass against it.

"How you doin', brother?" I ask him.

"Feelin' no pain. Well, not much, anyway. Smiley deadened that shit before he stitched me up. I'm fine."

"Glad to hear it." I'm not gonna make a big deal out of it, but Gunner getting shot threw me. He's my closest friend, in the club or otherwise. I've known him longer than I've known anyone outside my family.

"Looks like all in all, the run was a success," Gunner says with a grim smile.

"Yeah." I take a long pull off my beer. "Now we wait to see what the fallout is. Either way, it had to be done."

"Agreed." Gunner looks out at the bar. "The women sure look happy to have their men back," he observes.

"They do."

"Any reason why Sydney isn't here?"

Goddamnit, I should have known.

"Jesus fuck, is *everyone* gonna hound me about this?" I explode.

"We are if you're being a jackass," Gunner says evenly.

"Motherfucker," I snarl. "I'm done with this." I stand up and move to leave, but Gunner stops me.

"Look, brother," he half-slurs, the alcohol clearly beginning to interact with the painkillers he's taken. "I really like Sydney. She seems like a great chick. Plus she's got awesome tits. Even so, I wouldn't say a word about this if I thought for one second you were *really* done with her." He shakes his head and snorts. "But Jesus Christ, man, have you looked in a mirror lately? You look like shit. And you've been drinking like you're training for the Olympics of liver poisoning. You've always been kind of morose, but I've never seen you be such a goddamn martyr."

"Martyr?!" I'm *pissed*. If Gunner wasn't lying on this table right now recovering from being shot, I'd fucking shoot him myself.

"Yes, you goddamn martyr. Look at you. You're fucking miserable. How is this better for you? For *either* of you?"

My hand is clamped so tightly around the bottle I wonder if it might break. I try to loosen my grip, but I can't.

"I don't know which one of you did what," Gunner continues, oblivious to the fact that I'm thinking about punching him. "Or which one of you thinks the other one is in the wrong. But I know you. I know how you are. Shit, I've heard you say a thousand times that relationships are bullshit. That people are fooling themselves if they expect anything out of them. Even though you can look around you and see evidence you're wrong right in this room."

"You don't know what you're talking about," I snort.

"I know you're head over heels gone for Sydney. I know she's completely crazy about you. Jesus, Brick, are you really gonna just throw that away?" Gunner leans forward, looking me in the eye. "I tell you one thing, if I had a woman who felt that way about me, I wouldn't let her out of my sight. You brought that girl to this clubhouse for a reason," he murmurs.

"Why the fuck are you punishing both of you, for every other couple that didn't make it?"

I'm not, I want to say.

Fuck you, I want to scream.

You have no idea what you're talking about, I want to yell.

"You know I'm right, brother," Gunner says. "So you can hold on to your bullshit theories, and continue to be a recluse and an idiot. Or you can realize you deserve to be happy. And so does Sydney."

"Okay. You've said your piece," I bite out. "You done?"

"Not really," Gunner says cheerfully. "But I know that's all you're gonna listen to before you kick my ass, so it'll have to do."

I toss my empty bottle into the bin, go grab another beer from Jewel, and head upstairs to my apartment. I can't deal with anyone else's shit right now. It feels like the whole club is conspiring to tell me that I'm wrong about Sydney. They don't know what they're fucking talking about it. I mean, hell, I know she didn't lie to me on purpose to hurt me. She probably thought she was doing the right thing, fucked up as that is. How the fuck she got the idea that keeping information from me was protecting me, though, I have no goddamn idea. Especially when she was in danger.

Kind of like how you wouldn't have told her about this run today. Because you wouldn't have wanted her to worry about you. Even though you could have died.

That's different. There was nothing she could have done about this run. Why make her worry? If I'd known about that shit with Devon, I could have protected her. What happened at the coffee shop never would have happened.

It's not that different. You told her you couldn't trust her, because a lie of omission is still a lie. If that's the case, how could you expect her to trust you?

Fuck. All this shit is making my head hurt. I cross to the dresser, grab the mostly full bottle of whiskey that's sitting on the top, and throw myself onto the bed. I need to get drunk. I need sleep.

And mostly, I need to stop thinking about Sydney Banner.

36
SYDNEY

In the month since I last saw Gavin, I've been shocked to see that in spite of all the pain in my soul, and my heart — pain that makes me feel like I'm constantly struggling to move through water — life seems to go on for other people.

I texted him once or twice. Oh, who the hell am I trying to fool? I texted him at least ten times. He never replied. So, not only do I get to know he cared so little about me that he walked out once he saw the sordid past I dragged with me to Tanner Springs. I also get to feel the complete humiliation of me begging him to come back and him completely ignoring me.

Like a fool, I even considered going to the clubhouse. But I realized I no longer have the right to be there.

Sam stopped by the Golden Cup once to see me. I think she was trying to be nice. But it was just awful, and awkward, and the two of us were both trying to avoid the huge elephant in the room the whole time. She ended up getting her coffee to go and squeezing my hand, saying she was sorry and that she was sure things would work out between Gavin and me, somehow.

It's not going to work out.

For about a week, I was still afraid Devon would come back. But the days passed, and there was no sign of him, I eventually realized I was safe. And it's all because of Gavin.

I should have trusted him. I should have told him about Devon's texts from the beginning.

I will regret that decision for the rest of my life.

In blackjack, it's all about risk taking, and mitigating risk. Even when you're counting cards. If you're good at counting, you can beat the odds, but you always have to weigh that against the fact that people are watching all the time for card counters, and that even when you count, you still don't have the complete picture.

I've spent my life sizing people up. Taking risks, but not exposing myself. It's a game my father taught me. It's ingrained in me.

This? Letting myself be seen for who I am? Letting someone else in on my vulnerabilities? I'm not used to it. Even with Devon I never did it. I hate that I let myself be that vulnerable.

But I hate even more that *not* doing it with Gavin soon enough lost me the best thing I ever had.

In the weeks that follow, I interview and train new workers, many of whom are high school students referred by Hailey. I try not to pay attention to Beverly and Bradley's budding romance. Or Hailey and Teddy's.

It feels like relationships are blooming all around me. Almost like someone's playing a sick joke to mess with my head.

Beverly and Hailey both seem to sense there's something off with me. But they have the kindness not to ask too many questions.

I wish in a way that I hadn't hired any new people. Because the only thing keeping my mind off Gavin these days is work. And even though I really needed more staff, now I have less work to occupy my days. The hours stretch in front of me and I don't know how to fill the time between waking and going to bed. I'm practically jumping out of my skin.

Months ago, I came to Tanner Springs because I wanted a new start. A new life, away from Atlantic City. I wanted everything to be fresh.

But my past caught up with me, and ended up ruining what I had built anyway. Just not in the way I expected.

It's late afternoon on a Friday, and I'm getting ready to leave the shop for the day. Hailey and one of my new employees, Jamison, are going to be closing up tonight. Jamison is one of Hailey's classmates, and also plays guitar in a band. He's trying to convince me to start doing live music on the weekends, saying that the young people of Tanner Springs would come here in droves if I did.

"You'd only have to let them pass around a tip jar," he's telling me, his young face earnest. "You don't need to pay them at all. And think about all those people coming in and ordering coffee drinks and food. You'd be making serious coin!"

"That's a whole other ball game from what I'm doing now," I protest. "That means stocking a lot more baked goods, and maybe even sandwiches and bagels and things like that. I'm not sure I'm quite there yet." Truth be told, I *have* been thinking about starting to offer lunch items, but I've been putting it off. "And what about the crowds? I'm not sure having a bunch of rowdy high schoolers in here on a Friday night is a great idea."

Next to Jamison, Hailey snorts. "They're hardly going to be rowdy. Jamison's band plays folk and bluegrass music. The worst thing that could happen is someone will get their eye poked out by a flying banjo string."

The idea of taking on a new project sounds exhausting to me right now. I can barely function as it is, even as I find myself wishing I had something to occupy my mind twenty-four seven so I'd never have a chance to think about Gavin.

Still, I have to admit Jamison's idea is a good one. Most of the people who come to the shop in the late afternoons and evenings are kids their age anyway. It might be worth giving them something other than coffee to attract more of them.

"Tell you what," I say, leaning against the front counter. "I'm willing to give this a shot. But for now, let's keep it low key. We can do a Thursday night, starting sometime next month. No advertising to promote it. And no group. Just you, Jamison, on solo guitar. Let's see how the patrons like it. If it goes over well, then I'll think about making it a regular thing."

Jamison breaks into a face-splitting grin. "I can do that," he says.

"Okay," I nod. "We'll work out the details later. I'll look at the calendar for next month and get back to you on the date. And of course, this would be outside of your regular work schedule."

"Yeah, of course." He bobs his head in agreement. "And thanks, Sydney. This is a great opportunity."

Hailey pumps her fist and holds up her hand to high-five Jamison. I can't help but laugh; their excitement is contagious.

Behind me, the bell on the front door tinkles. I push away from the counter and stand up. "Okay, you guys, I'm gonna take off. Let me know if you need anything, but I'm assuming you've got this. Hailey, it's your job to train Jamison on how to close. If anything's left undone when I come in tomorrow, it's on you."

Hailey nods, but her eyes slip from mine to rest on a spot over my shoulder. They flick back to me uncertainly.

"Do you, um…" she stammers, "want me to take this order, or do you want to?"

I frown at her and turn around.

Facing me on the other side of the counter is Gavin.

"The usual," he says.

37
BRICK

Sydney's face goes pale when she sees me. Behind her, two high school kids are staring at me round-eyed.

"I know it's been a while, but I take it black," I prompt.

Sydney's eyes start to glisten. She clears her throat and opens her mouth to speak.

"I'm all out of blueberry muffins," she says throatily.

"No problem. Any kolaches?"

That gets a laugh. A soft, sad laugh, but a laugh nonetheless. I'll take it.

"Afraid not. They've been pretty popular. I need to start doubling my batches."

"Tell you what. I'll take a rain check on the coffee." My voice drops a notch. "I was wondering if I could talk to you for a minute."

"Um…" Sydney clears her throat and sniffles a little. "Sure." She glances back at the two kids. "Okay. You two are on your own," she says, and then turns back to me. "Let's go out front," she murmurs.

I stride to the front door and hold it open for her, letting it close behind me. Outside, she clutches her arms around her like she's cold. "What did you want, Gavin?" she asks, her eyes darting everywhere but at my face.

"I was wondering whether you were free later."

She half-sobs, half-laughs, and shakes her head.

"What?" I frown, confused.

"You've never actually *asked* me to do anything before. You've always just told me."

I can't help but chuckle. "Yeah. Well, I guess I'm turning over a new leaf."

For some reason, saying that makes Sydney's face darken. "Why are you here, Gavin?"

"I want to talk to you."

"What about?" Now that her initial surprise is subsiding, I can tell she's not going to make this easy for me.

"Not here." I lift my chin toward my bike, which is parked a few spaces down. "Come with me."

"Gavin," she sighs, looking impossibly sad. "I don't think this is a good idea."

"Sydney." My voice comes out half-broken, cracked and raw. "Please."

She pauses, and lifts her beautiful face to mine.

"Where do you want to take me?" she whispers.

"To the lake," I tell her. "I need to apologize, Sydney. But I don't want to do it here." I step forward and cup her chin in my hand. "I need to tell you some things. Please, give me a chance."

She flinches at my touch but doesn't move away immediately. She doesn't speak, either, and I can see on her face the fight that's taking place inside her.

"I'll drive myself there," she finally murmurs.

"When?" I'm almost weak with relief that she didn't say no. As long as she comes, that's all that matters.

"Now, if you want," she shrugs. "I'm done here for the day."

"You remember the way?" I ask her. She gives me a brief nod. I watch her as she turns and goes back inside the Golden Cup, and heads out back to her car. I know she said she remembers how to get to my place, but I'm afraid she'll change her mind halfway there, so I wait for her car to pull out onto the street and follow her out to my place.

When we get there, she climbs out of her car and wordlessly joins me on the front walk. I open the door for her and let her inside. She walks to the middle of the front room and stops, glancing around briefly.

"You put in new flooring," she remarks.

"Yeah. And that's about it since the last time you were here. I stopped work on the house."

"Why?" Her brow furrows.

"Well," I begin, "That's one of the things I wanted to talk to you about."

I offer her something to drink. She declines.

"There's still not a lot of places to sit in here," I admit. "But we could go out back."

Sydney gives me a slight nod and follows me outside to the deck. We sit down on the couch facing the lake, just like we did the first time I brought her here. She crosses her legs primly, and folds her hands in her lap. It's clearly a protective gesture, whether she's conscious of it or not. It's practically killing me not to touch her but it's obvious she doesn't want me to, so I make myself hold off for now.

Sydney doesn't speak at all; she just looks out at the water. I can tell she's waiting for me to start explaining myself. And she's right. It's time I tell her why I brought her out here.

"Sydney," I begin, savoring her name on my lips. I haven't allowed myself to say it since the day I broke things off with her. "I was pretty fucking angry with you, after what happened with Devon." I draw in a deep breath. "I know you tried to text me, and I just couldn't deal with talking to you. I wanted to make a clean break.

"Gunner knew a little of what happened. He told me I was being a fucking idiot when I said you and I were through. Somehow, without me telling him, he knew I was the one who ended it. He told me I was making a huge mistake. Gunner's known me a long time, and he knows I haven't had a lot of reason to believe relationships are meant to last. Oh, not from personal experience, exactly," I say, meeting her curious glance. "Just from seeing people betray each other, and lie to each other." I look out at the water. "I always told myself I wasn't going to fall into the trap of fooling myself like that. I thought I was happier alone. I didn't see the point in ruining the decent life I'd built for myself. I bought this house so I could live out my days here. My patch of land. Mine alone. That was enough."

I shift my body in her direction. My eyes lock on hers.

"And then I met you."

I reach out and take her hand. For a second, I think she's going to pull away, but she doesn't.

"I don't know how you got under my skin, Sydney. But I think I was a goner from the first time I ever walked into your shop. I'd never fallen for anyone before. I didn't even really notice it happening." I chuckle low in my throat. "One day, I woke up with you here, in my bed. I'd never brought anyone here before. And I realized I was in love with you."

Sydney's eyes fill with tears. Her lower lip quivers. I'm dying to pull her into my arms, to kiss that lip until it stops trembling, but I know it's not time yet. I still have to tell her the rest.

"I don't know how to act, Sydney," I continue gruffly. "I was out of my depth. I'd spent most of my life believing love is a fucking lie people tell themselves, and here I was head over heels crazy about you. I guess deep down, my subconscious was still looking for a way out. Looking for a way to prove that I was right all along. That love was a fairy tale for stupid people. And so, one day, I came to the coffee shop to surprise you at closing time. The front door was already locked, and I looked inside to see if you were there. And what I saw was, you kissing some guy in the hallway."

"You saw that?" Sydney gasps. "But it wasn't..."

"I know, baby," I say, interrupting her. "Obviously, I know now it wasn't what it looked like. Though at that moment I thought you were playing me for a fool. I was fucking furious. I started to drive away, but then luckily I figured out something didn't add up." I take a deep breath and let it out. *Confession time.* "When I installed those cameras in the shop, I hooked the feed to my phone, so I could keep an eye on you just in case." Sydney's eyes widen, a mixture of shock and dawning anger. "I know I should have told you that. I'm damn glad I did it, as it turns out, because that's how

I saw what was really going on with Devon. But I lied to you. A lie of omission." I shake my head, with a snort of laughter. "I lied to you. To protect you. And I broke up with you, for lying to me. Basically, I'm a jackass."

That gets a tremulous laugh from Sydney. "Well," she murmurs. "You do have a point there."

"I know, babe. And I'm sorry. For lying to you, but also for how I acted, through the whole damn thing. I almost missed the opportunity to save you because I didn't trust you. I saw you and Devon and thought the worst," I tell her. "I didn't give you the benefit of the doubt, even though everything I know about you should have told me to trust you. So, maybe you were right not to trust me with your whole story. Because look what I did the first time I saw something that I didn't understand. I immediately believed what I wanted to believe." I reach out and take her other hand in mine. "But I realize now that to protect you, I have to *trust* you. And to love you, I have to trust you. And I do, Sydney. I do trust you. Or at least, I want to. And I realize that's on me."

"Gavin," she whispers. The tears she's been holding back finally spill over. I let go of one of her hands, then reach up and wipe her eyes with my thumb. She leans her face into my palm, kissing it. A deep shiver runs through me at her touch.

"So, there's more I need to say," I tell her. This part scares me a little bit, and I almost don't say it. But it's the truth, and it's why I brought her here in the first place. And

I'm done holding myself back where Sydney is concerned. I'm going for broke, and if it doesn't work out, so be it.

"After things ended between us, I threw myself into redoing the floors here at the house. I decided to spend every spare moment working on the renovations, to take my mind off you. The thing is," I continue, "since I was doing the work myself, I had a hell of a lot of hours alone, with nothing but my thoughts to torture me." In spite of myself, I smirk. "That bastard Gunner's words kept coming back to me, ringing in my head with every pound of the hammer. Enough that I started doubting myself. And rethinking how I'd handled... well, pretty much everything.

"By the time I got done with the floor, I decided to take a break before I started the next project. I told myself that I was just losing steam and needed to give myself a breather. But that wasn't the reason.

"The reason was because even though I wasn't able to admit it to myself yet, this house didn't seem the same anymore." I reach up and softly stroke a wave of Sydney's hair. "I could still remember you here. Here on the back deck, looking at the lake. Sleeping in my bed, the red waves of your hair tumbling over the pillow. Sitting at that shitty card table with me having breakfast, dressed in nothing but one of my shirts."

My eyes lock on hers. This is it.

"Eventually I realized it. The house didn't feel right without you in it. And I couldn't do any more work on it until I knew whether you would be here to share it with me."

Sydney's been looking at me this whole time. When I say these last words, it takes her a moment to register what I'm saying. When she finally does, she blinks once and lets out a little squeak of surprise.

"Gavin!" she breathes. "Are you asking me to move in with you?"

"Not right away. Not if you don't want to," I say slowly. "But yeah. I'd like you to, as soon as you're comfortable with it." I glance back toward the house. "And in the meantime, I don't want to do anything more to it without your say so. It's going to be your house, too, so you should have it the way you like."

"Oh, my God." She looks slightly shell-shocked. "Okay, this is not how I expected this conversation to go."

"Babe," I rumble, pulling her into my arms. She doesn't resist, and my heart practically leaps out of my chest. "I don't have a lot of faith in a lot of things. But if there's anything the last few months have taught me, it's that I have faith in this. In *you*. And I'm done wasting my time living a life without you in it." I wait a beat. "If that's okay with you, that is."

Sydney bursts into laughter, so hard she snorts a little. It's the cutest damn thing I've ever heard. "I'm not sure I'm going to be able to get used to the Gavin who actually *asks* my permission before deciding things," she sighs, leaning back against my chest.

"Well, to be honest, I'm not sure I'd really take no for an answer," I tell her. "But hey, at least I'm trying, right?"

She sits up for a second, and turns to face me. Her eyes are glistening again, but this time I can tell the tears are happy ones.

"I love you, Gavin Malone," she breathes.

"I love you, Sydney Banner."

I kiss her long, and deep, and somehow we end up back in the house, on my shitty mattress on the living room floor. We make love slowly, taking our time, and with every kiss and stroke that takes her closer to the edge I tell her exactly how much I love her. I show her When I finally slide inside her I have to close my eyes for a second, it feels so good. Our bodies take over, everything falling away except the two of us. We come together, the two of us calling out to each other, and it's fucking amazing. Better than it's ever been.

And somehow, I trust — I *know* — it will just keep getting better.

EPILOGUE

SYDNEY

Six months later

"Hey, hot stuff! We're gonna be late if you don't hurry up. Hawk closed the garage early for a reason, you know!"

"I know, I know. Just give me a couple more minutes," Gavin mutters, peering into the engine of what he tells me is a 1963 Corvette.

"I brought you a change of clothes," I tell him. "I'll hang them in the bathroom for you."

"Thanks, babe. You're the best."

Glancing at my phone to check the time, I wander over to the main office to wait for him to finish. We're the only ones here, since Hawk closed the shop at noon today. It's a big day for him and his little family. Today's the day Sam and Hawk officially adopt little Connor. They've been waiting for this for a while and jumped through countless hoops. They even went to the courthouse a few months ago and got married, so there'd be absolutely no issues with having Connor become their son.

"Neither one of us really cares about a piece of paper," Sam told me at the time. "We know we're together forever, and that's all that matters. But we'll do whatever it takes to make sure Connor is ours, and I have to admit that it's best for his adoptive parents to be married. He's had so much instability in his young life. He deserves to know that his family is solid, and permanent."

I hear the hood of the Corvette slam shut, and a few minutes later Gavin comes into the office, all cleaned up and wearing jeans and a crisp dark blue button-down shirt that I ironed for him this morning.

"Damn," I murmur as he puts his arms around me. "It's a good thing you're mine, because if you weren't I'd have to put the moves on you."

Gavin's rumbling laughter envelops me like a warm cocoon. "Flatterer. You're just trying to get in my pants."

"True story," I admit.

"Lucky for you, flattery will get you everywhere," he growls as his mouth comes down on mine. Our tongues dance, and Gavin's hands reach down to cup my ass and pull my hips closer to his. Through the fabric of his jeans, I feel the hard insistence of his cock, and moan softly into his mouth as I angle myself to meet it. *Oh, God...* It's so good, like it always is. My arms reach up to wind around his neck, and Gavin lifts me until I'm resting hard against his cock, my legs around his waist.

"Okay," I gasp, tearing my mouth from his. "We have to stop now, or we'll end up having sex on Hawk's desk."

"That's the whole point," he murmurs against the pulse point of my throat.

"Gavin," I whimper. "We can't be late for this. It's important to Hawk and Samantha."

With a groan of disappointment, he lowers me and sets me down. "You pick the worst times to be rational, babe."

Gavin locks up the shop and we head out to my car, which we're taking because I'm wearing a dress and heels. Gavin drives us to the courthouse, and by the time we get there, most of Sam and Hawk's people are already assembled outside the hearing room. Almost all the Lords of Carnage are there, dressed more soberly than I've ever seen any of them. Several old ladies and children are there, too. Sam looks radiant and happy as she holds little Connor in her arms. He's been dressed in the most adorable little suit for the occasion, and he's holding onto his stuffed doggy, Woof.

When it's time, we all file into the hearing room and take our seats. Sam, Hawk, Connor, and their attorney sit down at the table facing the judge's bench. Sam leans over to say something to Hawk, and he puts his arm around her and kisses her softly on the forehead. It's so sweet I get a little teary at the sight, and when I sniffle softly, Gavin looks over at me and lovingly takes my hand.

The judge enters the room a few minutes later, and she looks momentarily a little startled at how many people are in the room to witness Connor's adoption. "Well," she remarks as she takes her seat. "It looks as though this family has a lot of support and love around them. That's an awfully good sign. I'm glad to see it."

The actual adoption goes off without a hitch. The judge reviews the paperwork, and asks both Samantha and Hawk to introduce themselves and testify as to why this adoption should take place. Samantha's voice quavers with emotion a little bit as she gives her testimony, and I don't blame her. I'm struggling to hold back tears the whole time. But it's Hawk's testimony that sends me over the edge.

"Your honor," he says after he's stated his name. "Connor is the sweetest, most loving little boy in the world. He deserves the absolute best parents there are. I'm a simple man, and I don't claim to be perfect. But I love this little boy with all my heart. I will do my best every single day of my life to make sure he knows he's loved and cherished by his mom and dad. And any weaknesses or shortcomings I might have, any mistakes I might ever make, my wife Samantha will make up for them, because she's the best mother I have ever seen."

Before I can stop it, a small sob escapes from my throat. The tears I've been fighting back fall down my cheeks, and I rummage in my bag for a tissue. Next to me, Gavin laughs softly and puts a tender arm around my shoulders.

At the end of the hearing, the judge signs the decree of adoption. The little family gets their picture taken with the judge. Sam and Hawk get copies of the paperwork to take home with them. And then, just like that, it's done. Connor is now Connor McCullough, the son of Hawk and Samantha McCullough.

"Congratulations, Sam and Hawk!" I cry in a wobbly voice when we're all back out in the lobby, surrounding the new family. "And Connor, too!"

"Thank you!" little Connor says. "I'm adopted now!"

"Yes you are, little guy," Hawk rumbles. Even his voice is a little gruff with emotion.

"Sam," says Jenna, cutting through the crowd. "We're going to go back to your place to get things ready for the party. Do you need me to pick up anything last-minute on the way?"

"No, I think we have everything there already," Sam answers. "Oh, but could you let Woof out in the back yard when you get there? I'm hoping he'll burn off some energy before the people come."

Woof, the real-life version of Connor's stuffed doggy, is a shepherd mix that came from Geno's dog Molly's litter. Sam and Hawk got Woof for Connor not long after he came to live with them, and the two of them are inseparable.

"Will do. Congratulations, mama," Jenna says, squeezing Sam's shoulder.

"Thanks, sweetie!" Sam beams at her. "This is a good, good day."

Back at Hawk and Sam's house, the party lasts for the rest of the day and only winds down when it's time for the youngest kids to be put to bed. One by one, people congratulate Sam and Hawk again and take off, leaving only a few of us sitting on their back patio in the moonlight.

"The old ladies really outdid themselves today," Gavin says as he pats his stomach, referencing all the food we made in preparation for the big day.

I shake my head and laugh. "I'm not sure I'll ever get used to you calling me your *old* lady," I say, wrinkling my nose at him.

Jenna pipes up. "Eh. Eventually it starts to sound different. Sweet, even. To me, anyway. Besides," she snorts. "One of these days I actually will be old, and then it'll fit. Until then, I'm fine with it."

It's about time for us to head out, but I don't want to leave Sam with a disaster in the kitchen, so I enlist Jenna to help me clean things up. Then the last of us say goodnight to the little family, and Gavin and I drive home to the lake.

"You tired, babe?" He asks me as we head up the front walk, his arm around me.

"A little," I say, "But I don't want to go to bed quite yet."

"Good," he says. "Because there's something I want to show you."

He unlocks the door and flips on the lights. In the main room, the newly timbered walls of the A frame are bathed in a golden glow. The cozy furniture I picked out makes the room look especially inviting tonight. Everything in here is all finished, except for one thing: our mattress is still there, lying in front of the fireplace until the new bedroom furniture gets delivered tomorrow.

Gavin takes my hand and leads me to the couch. I sit down and wait as he goes into another room and comes back with a couple pieces of paper.

"What's this?" I ask as he hands them to me. Frowning, I stare at the drawings on the top sheet. It's a diagram, and it only takes me a second to recognize that part of it is the floor plan of our house. But there's another piece added on, to one side.

"Now that most of the work on the main part of the house is done," he says, sitting down beside me, "I figured it's about time to think about an addition."

It's two stories, and would turn our bedroom into a master suite, and add on three other rooms.

"I bought this place just for myself originally," Gavin continues. "I never thought I'd need more room than I had, with just the one bedroom and the main area with the kitchen to the side. But obviously, I was wrong," he chuckles, pulling me into his lap. "I want this to be a place that we can be in for a long time. Maybe forever," he tells me. "You. Me. Our kids."

"Kids?" My heart starts to flutter. We've *never* talked about this before.

"Yeah. Kids," he grins. "I mean, I have to admit, having a family of my own wasn't something I'd ever even considered. I sure as hell never pictured me as some fucking little league coach or Boy Scout troop leader." Gavin reaches up to caress my jawline with his thumb. "But it turns out there were a lot of things I never considered, before I met you."

"Gavin," I begin, my eyes filling with tears for the second time that day. I try to say more but my throat closes up.

"Babe. You want kids, don't you?"

I laugh wetly. "Yes. Of course. But I guess I didn't think... I don't know. I didn't think you did, for some reason."

"I want everything with you, Sydney," he rasps. "Everything. Fifteen fucking kids. A houseful of craziness. The whole shebang."

The tears start to stream down my face. I'm grinning like an idiot. "I don't know about fifteen, Gavin, but maybe we could just start with… one?"

"You drive a hard bargain, babe, but one it is." He kisses my wet cheeks, one by one, and pulls me tight. "I love you, babe."

"I love you, Gavin," I whisper. Then, suddenly, I'm in the air, in his strong arms. I let out a squeal of surprise.

"What are you doing?" I cry as he carries me across the room.

"You said we could start with one," he answers. "So, let's get started."

Gavin sets me down on the mattress and moves over me. "This is the last time we'll fuck on this mattress," he rasps against my neck. "We should have some sort of ceremony for it."

"The last time?" I pretend to pout. "I thought you said you wanted to try for a baby, Malone. We have almost twelve hours until the furniture guys get here. Where's your sense of commitment?"

Gavin nips at my earlobe, sending a shiver through me. My arms go around his neck and I arch my head back. I cling to him tightly, my body already surrendering to his touch. His lips find the sensitive spot just behind my ear, and I reach up and fist one hand tight in his dark hair. He's wearing it longer now, and I love the way it feels to run my fingers through it.

"I can't wait until you're pregnant and your belly gets all big with my baby," he growls. "That's gonna be so fucking hot."

His lips travel across my skin, down to the hollow of my throat, and it's making my legs feel like jello. "You have too many clothes on," he complains. Reaching behind me, he finds the zipper on my dress and pulls it down in one fluid motion. I let go of his neck and let him pull it down off of me to my waist. He takes a long moment to stare at me in my lacy bra. "Fuck, you're beautiful," he tells me. He undoes the clasp in back and pulls it off me, then cups one of my breasts in his hand. He pinches the nipple gently, and I suck in a ragged breath and close my eyes. Then his warm lips begin to tease and suck, and a throbbing anticipation begins to build between my legs.

"Did you know," he says conversationally as he moves to the other breast, "that I've been thinking all day about what I wanted to do to you when we got home?"

"No," I begin to pant, my body stiffening with anticipation. "I didn't know that."

"I've been thinking about plunging my face between your legs and licking your pussy," he tells me, and lays me on the bed. "I was hard as a rock all through the adoption ceremony."

"Oh, my God, Gavin!" I laugh as he pulls on my skirt and I lift my hips to help him get it off. "That's terrible!"

"No court in the country would convict me," he murmurs thickly, sliding a finger underneath the thin fabric of my panties and finding the wetness there. I gasp as he grazes my clit, using my own slickness to tease me, then pulls it away and sucks my juices off his fingers. "Fuck. I'm so goddamn hard right now I'm about to come in my jeans, Sydney. But I'll manage to hold off somehow, because right now I need you to fuck my tongue."

He's up off the mattress, pulling off first shirt and then jeans, and then he's standing over me, his impressive erection bobbing in the light. I want to kneel, to take him in my mouth, but I know that when my man has decided what he wants there's no arguing with him. Instead, he slides down between my legs and spreads them wide. He kisses my lower lips, and I shudder. His tongue teases at me, just barely touching me, and I moan.

"Gavin, please," I whisper. "Don't make me wait."

"Greedy," he rumbles, and nips at the sensitive skin of my inner thigh. "I love that you're greedy."

I open my mouth to give him a smart answer, but then his tongue is sliding between my lips, finding my clit, and I freeze and thrust toward his mouth. He licks me in slow circles, knowing exactly how much pressure to use to make me crazy with need. I hear myself begin to whimper, my fists clutching at the sheets. Gavin's hands grip my thighs, pulling me closer to him, and then his tongue plunges inside of me, tasting me like I'm delicious and he can't get enough of me. He slides it out again and starts to swirl his tongue around my clit again, and now I'm so desperate I'm practically raising my whole lower body off the mattress.

"Gavin, oh, God…"

Gavin wraps his mouth around my clit then, sucking gently, my body goes rigid because it's so good and I want to come right now but I never want it to stop, and then, then, he flutters his tongue right *there* and I come, a deep, intense orgasm that shakes my whole body and makes my thighs quake uncontrollably.

I'm still coming when I feel Gavin shift and position himself above me. He slides the burning head of his cock against my slickened lower lips and my sensitive clit, and it's almost too much but it's so, so good.

He pushes against my entrance, and I draw in a sharp breath as I feel the hard thickness of him fill me. He keeps going, deeper and deeper, until he's in to the hilt, and even though it's a tiny bit painful at first, it also feels so good, so right. He grabs a pillow and lifts up my hips so he can put it under me, and the angle's a little different this way, a little tighter but also he can get even deeper like this.

"*Fuck*, Sydney," he groans. "Jesus fucking Christ you feel good. I'm going to come inside you, babe. I'm going to coat you with my come and we're gonna make a baby, and she's gonna look just like you."

Then he's thrusting, both of his huge hands gripping my hips and pulling me toward him as he drives into me. He's going so deep he's hitting this spot that's doing something amazing to me and I *moan* and I'm crying out *yes, yes,* with every thrust, and then Gavin lets go with one hand and slides his thumb across my sensitive clit and everything shatters as I come a second time and then a split second later he roars and explodes inside me.

I'm still shaking as Gavin pulls the pillow out from under me and pulls me up, then lays us both down, with him still inside me. He devours my mouth, both of us still breathing heavily, our hearts racing next to each other.

"Wow," I pant. "So that's what 'trying to make a baby' sex is like."

"I guess so," he agrees. "I like it."

"Gavin," I whisper. "Are you sure?"

"Sure of what?" He shifts his body slightly to look at me.

"Sure you want to start a family with me?"

"Yeah. I am." He pulls me closer and lets out a deep sigh. "I'm more than sure. It doesn't have to happen right away. But I'm ready for it to. I never used to think about the future before I met you, Sydney. But now that the future has you in it, I can't fucking wait for it to get here." Gavin chuckles. "I wasn't kidding when I said I want to see you as a sassy, sexy pregnant lady. And as the mom to all my kids. And hell, I want to see you as a gray-haired old lady. I want all of that."

"I want that, too," I breathe. "Except maybe not the part where I'm gray-haired and old."

He laughs and kisses my hair. "You're gonna be one sexy old lady, babe. I guarantee it."

I snuggle against his chest and close my eyes, trying to imagine what Gavin will look like when we're not just parents, but grandparents. A wave of love and gratitude hits me, so strong that it almost takes my breath away. I can't believe I get to spend my life with this man — this gorgeous, sexy, loving, complicated man. That I get to have him as the father of my children, and the grandfather to my grandchildren.

It's everything I never knew I wanted. And so much more.

THE END

ABOUT THE AUTHOR

Daphne Loveling is a small-town girl who moved to the big city as a young adult in search of adventure. She lives in the American Midwest with her fabulous husband and the two cats who own them.

Someday, she hopes to retire to a sandy beach and continue writing with sand between her toes.

Printed in Great
Britain
by Amazon